# Sweeter Than Sunshine
## OLIVIA MILES

~ Rosewood Press ~

ISBN 978-0692654958

SWEETER THAN SUNSHINE

Cover design by Go On Write

First Edition: March 2016

# Sweeter Than Sunshine

# Chapter One

Mary Harris liked to say there was an ice cream flavor for everyone. Her sister, Lila: mint chocolate chip. Her soon to be brother-in-law, Sam: cookies and cream. Her friend Hailey who ran the best café in Lincoln Park? Coffee bean, of course. And her ex, Jason, who had ceremoniously dumped her on New Year's Eve via text message and then had the nerve to suggest she cross the "friendship bridge" when she told him, also via text, where to go . . . He was straight up rocky road.

Mary sighed as she poured the cream, sugar, and vanilla into the ice cream machine. It was another quiet afternoon in the shop, and there had been too many of those lately. She'd prepared herself for a slow winter; after all, who really craved ice cream when it was ten below zero with three feet of snow on the ground? Spring was just around the corner—technically—but the forecast was calling for another eight inches by tonight, and the snowflakes had been falling steadily since daybreak. She should know, because she'd been up since then, trying to occupy herself with things like making coffee and watching a little morning television—anything to get her mind off that nagging thought: Had all this been a mistake?

She blinked away the question just as quickly as it formed. Ridiculous! Running Sunshine Creamery was the only job she'd ever loved—the only thing she'd ever really been passionate about, ever since she was a little girl sitting in the corner booth, watching her grandfather make waffle cones.

So things were slow. So her frozen eggnog and candy cane ice cream flavors had only been popular during the holidays . . . It was only a winter slump. She should embrace it. Use the time to come up with ten fun flavors for spring, maybe create some new signs for the windows, or just take a few weeks to relax. She hadn't done that in a while. In fact, Jason had said she didn't do it at all, or at least that was the excuse he'd given for breaking up with her when she'd finally dragged one out of him.

Mary sunk a spoon deep into a tub of raspberry chocolate truffle ice cream and brought it to her mouth. Savoring the sweet, smooth taste, she stared out the window as the snow continued to pelt the glass and coat the sidewalks. She had to admit, it was pretty, the way the tree branches were frocked, and the fire hydrants seemed to wear perfect white hats. But come tomorrow, when the city's traffic had taken its toll, the white and sparkling wonderland would be replaced with brown, murky slush, and grumpy Chicago residents who, like herself, were just ready for spring already!

The streetlight turned, and as the walk sign appeared, a kid darted across the street, straight toward her door. Mary guiltily dropped the spoon in the sink and straightened her shoulders, feeling downright embarrassed for her little burst of self-pity. She smiled eagerly as the boy pulled the door open and stepped inside, brushing snow from his hair as he glanced around the painfully empty room.

"Hello!" Mary said from behind the counter. From the smoothness of his cheeks to the weather-inappropriate canvas sneakers he wore, she pegged him to be around sixteen, seventeen at the most. Cookies and cream, she decided, and then waited to see if her hunch was right.

Instead the kid looked at her and asked, "Restroom?"

Mary blinked as the smile slipped from her face. Careful not to overreact, she swallowed and said, "End of the hall."

*Maybe he'll want a sundae when he returns*, she told herself, as he disappeared through the door. What kid can resist ice cream?

Outside the wind howled, forcing the door open a few inches. Mary frowned. Who *couldn't* resist ice cream in weather like this?

Moment later, she heard the flush of a toilet, the running of water. Quickly, she tried to look busy by straightening some glass sundae bowls.

"Thanks," the kid muttered, his shoulders hunched as he beelined for the door.

Mary tried to hide the swell of disappointment that was building in her chest. "Anytime," she lied. She had a strict policy about this type of thing, usually. Desperately, she grabbed a coupon from the top drawer near the cash register and waved it with forced cheer. "Buy one cone, get half off the second."

The kid hesitated at the door and then, with great reluctance, reached out a hand for the small slip of paper Mary had designed and printed herself, one equally quiet day a few weeks ago. She kept the smile frozen to her face until he had left, telling herself surely he'd hold on to it, come back with a friend, spread the word around school, until she spotted him dropping her cute little handmade coupon into the overflowing bin on the corner across the street.

Well! Mary counted to ten and talked herself out of marching across the snowy crosswalk, reaching into the trash, and salvaging her hard work. Instead, she plucked a fresh spoon from the canister and indulged in a hefty scoop of cookie dough—without the ice cream. Because yes, it was freezing outside, the wind was picking up, and the hair on her arms was still on end from the icy blast that had ripped through the door when that ungrateful coupon tosser had left.

Mary rubbed her arms, pressing her wool sweater a little closer to her skin. She hated to turn up the heat—just thinking of those bills made her stomach heave—but she couldn't stand it much longer.

With a glance at the clock, and a silent promise to herself that it was okay to turn the sign a little early tonight, what with a blizzard and all, she wandered to the back storage room to check the thermostat.

Her step slowed as she detected the sound of running water, and, pinching her lips, she marched to the bathroom, cursing under her breath when she thought of how quick that boy was to dismiss her efforts, how nice she had been to break her own policy and let him use the facilities, and flicked the light switch. The room was still, the sink off, and with a sudden pounding of her heart, Mary pivoted on her heel and stared with growing dread at the storeroom door, where, God help her, a trickle of water was seeping through the crack at the base.

She crossed the hall and flung open the door, her mouth gaping as her gaze shot up to the ceiling where water had formed a large brown stain on the freshly painted surface. A thick, icy drop hit her square in the eye, and she brushed it away quickly, her eyes dropping to scan the shallow puddle she was standing in, and the soggy, industrial-sized bags of sugar and chocolate chips that she kept back here. Another drop hit her on top of her head, and, when she looked up again, her cheek, and that's when she decided her optimism had officially expired for the day.

Mary balled her fists and screamed. She screamed because she could. Because there was no one around to hear her. Because she'd been holding her frustration inside since the first of the year, when her Santa Sundae had officially stopped luring customers and spring was still nearly three months away. It had been festering and bubbling and building inside her and now, now just weeks before the final arrival of spring, there was a damn blizzard, and now she finally had a real reason to just let it all out. She screamed again, and then, realizing how good it felt, screamed a little louder. She could have screamed all day, except for the fact that every second she spent doing that, the big, rusty, scary patch on the ceiling grew a little bigger.

She thought fast. She had to turn off the water. When the contractors were here last summer helping her spruce up the place, they'd shown her how to do that. Of course, she hadn't really bothered to pay much attention to the boring stuff, not when her mind was racing with new ideas for the menu, and struggling to decide between fourteen different shades of pastel-colored paint for the bathroom . . .

She sloshed to the utility room door at the back of the storage room and began frantically looking for something that would jog her memory. There were all sorts of knobs and switches. One did look a bit familiar . . . She blinked, hovering her hand just above it, and then, deciding she didn't have much of a choice, gave it a good hard turn.

Okay, so the place hadn't blown up. That was a good sign.

What wasn't a good sign, she realized when she scurried back into the storage room, was that the water continued to drip.

Deciding not to let herself think about what she might have just turned off, she bit her lip, said a silent prayer, and cranked the handle in the opposite direction, back in place.

Still no explosion. She blew out a sigh. See, she could handle this.

Except that she still didn't know where the water shutoff valve was. Yes, that's what it was called. A water shutoff valve.

She stopped. Told herself to calm herself down, and tried to focus. It was no use.

Reaching into her back pocket for her phone, her finger paused over the digits. You didn't exactly call emergency for this type of thing, did you? The contractors didn't answer her calls even when they were being paid a pretty sum by the hour.

It was times like this when she wished she still had a dad. Or a grandfather. Or a boyfriend . . .

She thought of Jason, and his perfectly random text message he'd been planning for God knew how long, timed on a day she'd been looking so forward to. Then she thought of the carefully wrapped present she'd already purchased for Valentine's Day, even if she had been getting a bit ahead of herself, which was now resting neatly at the bottom of her garbage chute.

She didn't need a man. Not to hold her at night. Not to tell her how to shut off a damn water valve.

She could do this. She set a hand on her hip, thought long and hard, studied another knob for a few minutes, and, finally, turned it.

Within a few minutes the water had stopped dripping, and in less than an hour she had managed to mop most of the puddle from the floor. Two urgent voice mails to the contractor later, and not a customer in sight, Mary decided that it was officially time to call it a day.

*

He'd done it again. Ben Sullivan shook his head and muttered under his breath as he fished his transit card from his wallet and turned back to the "L" station, his steps feeling heavy as he climbed once more to the platform opposite the one he'd just exited.

He turned his coat collar to the wind and craned his neck down the dark tracks, frowning at the lack of headlights in the distance. He should be home by now. Home in the house he and Dana had moved into eight years ago, the one with the kitchen he'd personally designed and installed, the one with the sunroom addition he'd built four years ago. The one with his daughter sleeping upstairs.

Instead, he was in for another long night in front of the television, with a frozen pizza and an ice cold beer while the nanny put his daughter to bed, and his ex-wife focused on the real love of her life: her job. He squinted into the distance, through the heavily falling snow, past the restaurants and bars and buildings he had memorized over time, thinking of how close the house was, and how inconceivable it was that he didn't live there anymore, and never would again. That an entire part of his life was now just a chapter, closed and shelved, distant and murky, and almost impossible to believe had ever once been real.

Ben jammed his hands into his pockets and turned back to the tracks, straightening when he noticed the lights appear in the distance. The train slid to a stop, its doors opening in front of him, and he stepped into the brightly lit compartment once more, eager to get away from his past and back to his new reality. The one he was still struggling to accept, even if he knew it was for the best.

When they'd first separated, Ben had assumed the apartment he'd rented would be temporary. It was small, but with a second bedroom for Violet on the nights she stayed with him, an efficient enough kitchen, given that he didn't cook, a close walk to the train, and a carefully calculated three stops from his then soon to be ex—just far enough so he didn't have to worry about running into her; just close enough so he could easily pick up his daughter on his scheduled nights and weekends. He'd assumed that by the time the divorce was finalized, he'd be back on his feet, establishing roots again, hell, maybe even dating.

So much for that.

And as for the apartment . . . Somehow he just hadn't dragged himself to look for something better, and the longer he stayed in it, the easier it was just to go with the flow instead of pushing for something more. After all, that's how he'd ended up in this mess, wasn't it? By pushing for something more? His sister told him his complacency was due to the fact that he was secretly hoping he would get back together with Dana, but she couldn't have been more wrong. It was more that he still couldn't believe his life had come to this, and picking up the pieces, starting over properly, meant accepting that it had.

The wind raced through the warm train car when the doors opened again, and Ben hurried the four blocks to the tall brownstone building that still felt foreign and strange, more like a temporary hotel room than an established residence. He collected the mail and jogged up the steps to the third-floor landing, keeping his head bent and his eyes forward. His sister had thoughts on this, too. Claimed he was becoming a hermit. Said at thirty-three he was too young to close himself off to the world. Maybe he was. But he just wasn't ready to let anyone back in just yet.

He reached the top floor and quickly slid his key in the lock, eager to close the door behind him and tune out the world for a bit, but a sudden noise made his hand still. He paused, waiting to see if he'd just imagined it, but there it was again, only louder this time, as distinct as the freckle next to his left eye. A woman was crying. No, not crying. Wailing. A woman was wailing. And it wasn't just any woman. It was his neighbor. The neighbor he had been dutifully avoiding since she moved into the building two months ago and dared to toss him that big, friendly smile and say hello. He'd all but frozen on the word, grunted something of a response, and vowed to keep his distance going forward. A girl like her would have made him cross a crowded room back in his single days. But he'd changed since then. A bad marriage could do that to you.

Ben cursed under his breath and hurried with his key as the sound of a nose blowing filled the small hallway. But damn it, he wasn't quick enough. From behind him he could hear the turning of the locks over a few determined sniffles, and then a voice, small and sweet, saying, "Excuse me?"

Ben closed his eyes. He'd seen the sign on the stairwell door. The petition for a proper recycling program for the building—no doubt she'd want to talk to him about it, ask why he hadn't signed it yet, if he perhaps didn't believe in recycling.

Since moving into the building, the girl across the hall was full of perky ideas for improvement. There had been the suggestion of the community garden on that back patch of dirt one might call a yard, an initiative for a "spruced up" laundry room in that cave of a basement, and the call for "beautifying" the front entryway, whatever that meant. And who could forget the invitation to an ice cream social to "get to know your neighbor." When one sign came down, another went up. Next thing, she'd probably be suggesting a progressive dinner! Just another reason he'd been sure to avoid her.

He turned, raising what he hoped to be a polite but not entirely interested eyebrow and stared flatly at the girl across the hall. She was a several years younger than him, probably in her mid to late twenties, and she was pretty, not that it mattered. He had to admit he was slightly curious to discover that little miss sunshine had actually been crying, but he resisted the urge to ask the reason. It wasn't his business, and he knew from experience that when things were rough, it was better to be left alone.

Her big brown eyes were puffy, swollen, and red rimmed. He swallowed, suddenly feeling like a jerk. In all the time they'd share the third floor, he'd barely spoken to her, and that was only in response to her initiation. He didn't even know her name. Giving her a name would be making her real, making her someone he'd have to acknowledge, chat with about the weather—and all that would make it entirely too difficult to overlook the way her auburn hair bounced at her shoulders and her pink lips pouted when she stood at the mailbox, inspecting the day's letters.

Only right now that hair was sort of standing on end, half pulled back in a messy ponytail, the rest frizzing out in every direction. Her cheeks were pink, her eyes bright and watery, and damn it if that didn't make her even more attractive.

"I was down near the mailboxes today, and I noticed—"

He held up a hand. "Look, I know this recycling thing is important to you, but it seems to me that you have all the signatures you need. I have a lot on my plate right now, and while I support the cause, I just don't have time to pitch in with all these little building initiatives."

The girl's eyes flashed in surprise and then narrowed a fraction. "That isn't the reason I wanted to speak to you, actually, but now that you mention it, thank you for letting me know. I'll be sure to include a note on my next *little building initiative* that it pertains to everyone but you." Her nostrils flared slightly as she crossed her arms over her chest.

Ben dragged out a sigh. He suddenly missed Bonnie terribly. Bonnie, the fifty-some-year-old woman who had lived across the hall for years before he'd come along, who was content to wave a simple greeting, who needed nothing more from this world than her tabby cat and her boxed wine. Bonnie didn't knock on his door. Or create petitions. Bonnie might not have been beautiful, as her replacement was, but oh, she had been the ideal neighbor.

He suddenly wondered what had happened to Bonnie, and shame bit at him when he realized he hadn't even said a proper good-bye.

Maybe his sister was right. Maybe his life was unraveling.

"Look, I didn't mean it like that, I just meant that I—"

Now it was her turn to hold up her hand, even if it did clutch a balled up and soggy-looking tissue. "I know, I know. Don't worry. I'm not here to harass you into being neighborly. I wanted to let you know that I received some mail for you. At least, I think it's for you. It has your apartment number on it, but it's addressed to someone named Violet." She tipped her head in question, and Ben felt his body stiffen in defense.

"Yes, that's for me, then. I mean, for Violet."

The girl's eyebrows pinched slightly. "I don't know why I thought you lived alone. But then, I just moved in and I'm rarely here on evenings and weekends."

*And when you are here, you're busy making petitions*, Ben thought to himself.

The girl disappeared behind the door for a minute and came back with a small box in her hands. It was the necklace he had ordered for Violet's birthday. "Thank you," he said gratefully.

"Well, that's what neighbors are for," the girl said, and with a purse of her lips, began closing her door.

"Wait," Ben said, and then clamped his mouth shut, cursing himself. He knew the type. Outgoing. Happy. Fun. Eager to be involved, to rally people together. She was looking for some big happy family, and he . . . well, he'd had that. Lost it. "Is . . . everything okay?"

Well, now he'd done it. Gone and done the right thing. Next thing he knew she'd be stopping by to borrow sugar, not that he had any.

She blinked at him a few times, her cheeks reddening. "It's just . . . It's been a bad day." She gave a watery smile.

Ben gave a small grin. "I've had a few of those myself," he admitted.

Her smile was a little easier. "I'm Mary, by the way."

"Ben," he said, but she was already nodding.

"I know."

Of course she did. She'd swept into the building with an eager smile, full of cheerful hellos and good-nights, a friend to everyone from the garden level up through the second floor within a week. Alarm bells started to ring in his head. *Time to leave, Ben. Time to go. End this politely, step inside your apartment, and shut the door behind you. And lock it.* "Well, good night, then. And thank you."

"As I said. That's what neighbors are for." She smiled, a sight so sweet, with those full pink lips and rosy cheeks and bright eyes that he felt himself waver.

Ben clutched the box tighter in his hand, thinking of his daughter, the tears in her eyes when he'd moved out, and tightened his resolve. There were lots of pretty girls in this city. Didn't mean he was looking.

He only needed one girl in his life from now on. And she was five years old.

*

Could this day get any worse? Mary stared at her reflection in her bathroom mirror and watched as another tear slipped down her mascara-stained cheek.

Nope, she decided. It couldn't.

Had she known that she looked like something out of, well, a horror movie, she might have thought twice about opening the door and handing over the package to her oh so hot and oh so aloof next-door neighbor. Here she'd convinced herself that her cheeks were probably just nicely flushed from crying, and it hadn't felt right to withhold the package, especially when she rarely crossed paths with the man and didn't know when she would again. She didn't like the idea of knocking on his door— he hadn't been very receptive the first time she'd done that, giving her a long, borderline menacing stare that made her heart speed up and her words stumble, when all she'd been hoping to ask him for was the code to the storage locker in the basement—and not knowing the contents of the package, it didn't seem responsible to leave it on his doormat.

So instead she'd done the right thing. And made a complete fool of herself in the process.

She sniffed again and then flicked off the light. Oh, well. So the guy was good looking and no doubt thought she was unstable or something. He was also, she knew from experience, a total jerk. And hadn't she dealt with enough of those lately? It didn't matter what he thought of her. Not when she didn't think too highly of him herself.

Besides, he apparently lived with someone named Violet. He was probably married.

Mary wandered into the kitchen and filled the kettle

for tea. Then, on second thought, she plucked a bottle of wine from the fridge instead. One drink, she thought. One drink and then she'd sit down with her bills, clean up this apartment she could barely pay for, clear up this mess she'd created for herself.

On the bright side, she thought, she'd been so busy worrying about the shop all day, she'd barely even thought about Jason.

She rewarded herself with a piece of chocolate for that. Maybe there was hope for her yet.

# Chapter Two

Everything always looked brighter in the morning, at least that's what Mary always believed. But today, the sun was stubbornly hiding behind thick grey clouds, and the loud, determined grind from the snow plow woke her long before dawn.

Mary was the first customer of the day at Corner Beanery, the Lincoln Park café run by her friend Hailey Wells. She stomped the snow off her boots on the mat in the window-framed vestibule and then pushed open the door into the warm and cozy room, still shivering the last of the winter chill off her shoulders.

"It's a cold one out there!" Hailey remarked as she set a plate of oversized blueberry muffins on the counter.

Mary tried not to let her expression show just how much this observation bothered her. While the snow had stopped—for now—the temperature had dropped, and the wind was fierce. Mary had worn a long-sleeved shirt under her wool turtleneck sweater, but even her down parka, scarf, hat, and gloves did little to keep the warmth inside.

Of course, the fifteen-minute walk hadn't helped either.

She approached the counter, her eyes drifting over the croissants and scones piled high in wicker baskets. A cup of coffee would do her good. Not that she hadn't already had two cups this morning while she compiled her list of plumbers to call first thing this morning, just in case her regular contractor didn't give her an answer she liked. She patted her pocket, making sure the list was still there. Surely one of them would offer a quote she could afford. If not . . . Her heart began to pound. Well, she'd just call another.

"You're in early today," Hailey commented as she poured Mary's favorite blend of coffee into a mug and handed it to her.

"Oh, the plows woke me up early." Mary handed over a few dollars and dropped the change into the tips jar. Ever since she started working at Sunshine Creamery, she knew how far a tip went for morale. Even if it was just a few dimes, the intent always lifted her spirit a bit and reminded her why she was doing this in the first place.

Most people she knew would balk at the thought of taking over their grandfather's ice cream parlor. But Mary couldn't have imagined it any other way. And she knew her grandparents couldn't have either. They'd built that place out of love and hard work, and even if they hadn't gotten rich, they were happy.

She could only begin to wonder what they would think of her now. She closed her eyes for a moment, trying to picture their smiles, the sound of their voices. Sunshine Creamery had been in a rut when she'd taken it over. It hadn't been lucrative for them, and no doubt they'd had their share of struggle, too. It couldn't have survived much longer, even if Gramps was around, but even then, he'd begged her to hold onto it, to see it through, keep it going.

She'd make it work; she'd promised herself that. She'd promised her grandfather, too.

"How's business?" Hailey asked conversationally as she started foaming milk for a customer's latte.

"Oh . . ." Mary untied her wool scarf and settled onto a counter stool near the espresso machine. "A bit slow, but it's winter, so I expected that."

"Well, spring is almost here," Hailey said brightly, and Mary gave a weak smile in return. She kept her back firmly to the window. She didn't need to see just how far from the truth that statement felt. "I have some interesting news, actually," Hailey offered.

Mary perked up, happy to shift topics. "Oh? A new guy in your life?"

Hailey barked out a laugh. "More like a new girl in my life. My cousin Claire is staying with me for a while."

Hailey leaned across the counter and whispered, "She was supposed to move to San Diego with her boyfriend. She quit her job, subleased her apartment, everything. The guy broke up with her a week before the moving trucks arrived."

"That's terrible!" Mary shook her head. "And here I thought I was the one with bad luck with men."

Hailey lifted an eyebrow. "Name someone who doesn't."

Mary thought for a second. "Lila," she said, thinking of how happy her sister was with Sam, cozily sharing a beautiful new apartment and walking together to their small advertising agency each morning. Their entire day, from morning to night, was a team effort.

She and Jason had never been part of a team. He couldn't understand why she had to work weekends, why she cared so much about Sunshine Creamery. His eyes would glaze over when she talked about new flavors.

It hurt. It still did.

Hailey started an espresso for the next customer. "You're forgetting that it wasn't always so wonderful with Lila and Sam."

Mary tipped her head. "True."

"What's this about Lila and Sam?" Lila called out from the doorway. Mary turned to see her sister, her cheeks flushed from the cold, her grey eyes bright with what she knew to be happiness.

"We were just talking about how unlucky we are with

men," Mary said. "But then Hailey pointed out that you and Sam found your way back to each other. There may be hope for us all."

Only she wasn't really so sure about that anymore. And she wasn't so sure she was willing to take the risk to find out, either.

"So I restored your faith in men, did I?" Sam grinned as he appeared over Lila's shoulder.

Mary had to smile. Sam was as charming as he was handsome. It was easy to see why Lila had never gotten over him after he'd broken her heart years back, when she was still living in New York. She watched as Sam bid his hello and good-bye in one greeting, claiming an early conference call. He gave Lila a kiss on the lips before darting back out into the snow, and Mary couldn't help it, she felt a pang of . . . longing. The way Sam looked at her sister, you'd think they wouldn't see each other again for hours, days even, when in fact, Lila would be down the street at their office in about twenty minutes.

She took a sip of her coffee. No use feeling sorry for herself. From where she stood, men were nothing but trouble, and she had enough of that on her plate, thank you very much.

"You look a little tired this morning," Lila commented after she'd told Hailey her order.

"Gee, thanks." But Mary knew her sister hadn't meant any harm. She was tired, she couldn't deny it. And she probably couldn't hide it forever, either. She looked out the window at the people bundled in hats, scarves, and coats on their walk to the bus stop, their shoulders hunched against the bitter wind, and winced. She'd be lucky to see one customer today.

"You know I'm just concerned. Is the shop still keeping you so busy?" Lila added cream and sugar to her coffee, blissfully unaware of Mary's troubles, and, if Mary had anything to do with it, it would stay that way.

She knew that Lila and Sam were the two people that could probably help the most, given their expertise in advertising as well as their financial position, but Lila had already helped enough, and it just didn't sit right with Mary to lean on her sister anymore. Lila was busy planning her wedding, enjoying her time with Sam, getting her new agency off the ground. No, this was Mary's problem alone. She had been the one who insisted they find a way to keep the family ice cream parlor, and Lila had supported that dream by offering an investment to get it running again. To tell Lila how bad things had been lately would be like a slap in the face. Mary couldn't do it. She felt sick at the mere thought.

"Oh, a bit slower than usual, but it's giving me time to come up with fresh flavors for the summer. What do you think about cherry cheesecake?" she asked, hoping her smile didn't look as strained as it felt.

"Sounds delicious!" Lila said. "But I might have to cut down on my ice cream consumption if I'm going to fit into a wedding dress!"

"Have you found one yet?" Mary asked. They'd been

to many stores, but Lila was still undecided as of their last shopping trip.

Lila shook her head. "There's time."

*Not much*, Mary thought, considering the wedding would be at the start of summer. It seemed so soon and yet, in her situation, so very far away.

By June, people would be lining up to sample her flavors; children would be licking cones on the benches she set up on the sidewalk, couples would be stopping by for a dessert after their dinner. But by June, there was a real possibility she might already be out of business.

She glanced at her watch. Her contractor had given her a two-hour window that started in twenty minutes. It would be quicker to take the bus to the shop, but she needed the walk, and besides, every dollar counted right now.

She looked guiltily at her coffee cup.

"I'd better run, actually," she said, sliding her gloves back on her hands.

"So soon?" Lila looked puzzled. "But you don't open for hours."

"Oh, you know me," Mary said quickly. "I thought of five new flavors just sitting here that I want to try out before the customers start flooding in." Her cheeks were hot and she struggled to make eye contact with her sister or Hailey as she walked to the door, waving back at them.

She didn't calm down until she was two blocks away, the cold air giving her a new perspective. Who knew, maybe she was being fatalistic. Maybe the contractor would tell her it was a quick fix, no biggie. Maybe she was worrying for nothing.

She crossed her fingers inside her pockets. Maybe.

*

Ben flicked off his computer monitor and leaned against his chair to stretch his back. It had been a long work day, but a busy one, and he was grateful for that. What he wasn't grateful for were the worried glances from his father's assistant, or the lunch break phone call from his sister, who had the name of yet another therapist he might want to try, since, she'd told him more than once, it wouldn't work for her to treat him herself.

As if he'd ever asked for her professional opinion.

He groaned. Working for a family business had its benefits, but he longed to get home, even if it was a far cry from his former one, and pretend for a few hours that everything was okay, that his wife hadn't surprised him with a divorce, that the life he'd planned and thought he'd been living hadn't all shattered before his eyes.

"Heading out?" his father asked when Ben stopped by his corner office.

Ben nodded, and let his eyes drift out the windows onto the illuminated Chicago skyline, the same view that had enthralled him as a kid when he'd come by the office with his mother. Sullivan Construction had occupied this space since his father first started the company in the seventies. It was nice to know that unlike other areas in his life, some things didn't change.

"You should come for dinner soon," his father continued. "Your mother would like that."

Ben nodded noncommittally. No doubt his mom had heard about another single daughter from one of her friends in bridge club. The last time he'd driven to the suburbs for a family meal, he'd been surprised to find a thirty-year-old blond woman with a bright smile and hungry eyes, who just happened to stop by for a drink. He'd spent the entire evening dodging his mother's meaningful stares from across the table, made a polite excuse and an early exit.

His phone vibrated against his leg. Without reaching into his pocket, he cursed under his breath. "That will be Emma. Again."

"Don't be so hard on your sister," his father remarked. "She's just worried about you."

Ben gritted his teeth before he said something he'd regret. It had been years since the split. What would it take to make his family start treating him like normal again? Ben's lips thinned as he settled on the answer to this question. A woman. They thought that all he needed to be happy again was the love of a good, strong woman.

They couldn't have been more wrong.

"Well, I'll see you in the morning." Ben held up a hand and wandered down the hall, nodding good night to his coworkers on his way to the elevator bank.

By the time he reached the lobby, his phone was ringing again. Emma could be persistent. Chances were she wouldn't stop trying until she'd reached him.

He dragged out a sigh as he pulled the device from his pocket, preparing himself to firmly remind his sister that she didn't need to check up on him so often, and that he wasn't one of her patients, when he saw the name on the screen.

He stopped walking, and barely even noticed when the crowd gathered around him, one man knocking his shoulder as he hurried to the revolving doors. There were three missed calls. And none of them were from Emma.

They were all from Dana. His ex-wife.

*

For the second night in a row, Ben exited the "L" at his old stop—only this time it wasn't by mistake. The snow was still falling steadily as Ben rounded the corner onto the street he'd once lived, dusting his shoulders as he quickened his pace. Dana had been cryptic on the phone, only reassuring him that Violet was fine, but that he needed to come over. Tonight. And no, it couldn't wait.

He stopped for a second to take in the pristine line of brick townhouses tucked behind iron gates, some old, some, like his, renovated from the ground up, and then forced one foot in front of another, his body leading his path on autopilot, his mind trailing.

Swinging open the gate, he jogged up the salt-covered steps to the large front door and rang the bell, wondering, as he waited, if Dana had shoveled the path herself, or if there was someone else in the picture, someone neither she, nor Violet, had mentioned. Jealousy hit him hard. He'd never get used to not seeing his daughter every day. It wasn't supposed to turn out like this.

"Daddy!"

Ben felt his chest swell as his little girl ran down the long hallway toward him, arms spread wide, her long, dark hair bouncing against her back. He crouched down to greet her, feeling the thud of her body as she hit his chest and her arms flung around his neck. He scooped her up, twirled her once around in the air and gave her a kiss on the cheek. "How's my girl today?"

"I'm good, but Daddy, guess what?"

Ben gently set her on the floor and stared into her big, earnest eyes that were the exact shade of blue as his own. "What?"

"Billy B. got in trouble today. Again." She pinched her little lips together and folded her arms across her chest.

Ben knew all about Billy B., not to be mistaken with Billy P. who was one of the nicer boys in Violet's kindergarten class, at least according to Violet. "Uh-oh. What did he do?"

Violet put her pointer finger to her lip and tipped her head in thought. Seconds ticked by until she finally announced, "I forget!" and bounded off toward the kitchen.

Ben sighed. No doubt Dana was back there, preparing dinner or cleaning up. Dread filled him as he walked to the back of the house, passing the formal living and dining rooms on his left. He rarely came in here anymore; usually Violet was picked up and dropped off outside of the house. It was easier this way, for both of them. After all, the house wasn't his anymore; it had gone to Dana in the divorce. But still, as he passed the rooms he couldn't help but skirt his gaze to notice if much had changed.

It felt oddly the same. He wasn't so sure if that was a good thing or not.

At the back of the house, the hall ended in a big, gourmet kitchen that opened onto the informal family room. Cartoons were playing on the television mounted above the fireplace, and sure enough, Dana was sitting at the granite-topped island.

Ben frowned and stopped a healthy distance from her. She was still pretty, objectively speaking, but his feelings for her had faded with time. Now when he looked at her, he saw two things: the mother of his child, and the woman who had thrown away the best chance at happiness any of them had ever had.

He resisted the urge to fold his arms across his chest. "You said this was too important to discuss on the phone. What's up?"

Dana shifted her eyes to the family room, where Violet was curled up on the sectional sofa, clutching her favorite stuffed bunny, engrossed in the children's program.

"It's my job," Dana said in a low voice.

Ben stifled a sigh. "Of course. Your all important job."

"I don't expect you to understand," she replied crisply.

"Then we're in agreement there." Ben fought back his temper. He and Dana would never agree on most things, her job prioritization being one of them. He loved that she was smart, cool headed, and ambitious. What he didn't love was the way she constantly put her public relations career before anything—and anyone—else. "What is it now? A change in schedule? Something with the nanny? If you need me to start picking Violet up from school, that's not an issue."

His job was more flexible, thanks to the family business. She knew it. She'd taken advantage of it, too.

"It's a transfer actually," Dana said after a pause.

Ben felt the blood drain from his face. He stared at Dana, waited for his pulse to resume a somewhat normal speed, and finally repeated, "A transfer."

"It's more of an assignment, really. Long term. They need me to take over the London office, until they find a suitable replacement. You remember Alan? Well, he left, and . . ." She caught his eye. "Anyway, they need me there."

Just like they'd needed her in the Los Angeles office once. "For how long?"

"I don't know. It could be a month. It could be six."

More like six if history proved anything. Or, maybe they'd decide to keep her on. He wouldn't be surprised. Ben was nodding, trying to digest this, but his throat felt like it was closing up. He ran a hand through his hair in agitation. It was still wet from the melting snow. "And

Violet?" he asked sharply.

"That's why I needed to see you tonight. They need me right away, and seeing as I don't know how long I'll be there, I think it's best that Violet stays with you, at least until everything is settled."

Ben didn't blink for several seconds. He was shaking, he realized. With relief, and with fresh anger so deep he wasn't sure he could control it. Everything would be settled, all right, and for good this time. Violet needed a stable, secure home, and he was going to be the one to give it to her.

He glanced to the family room, where Violet was giggling at the show. He would control his feelings right now. For her sake. All of it was for her.

"So you're just going to fly to London and leave Violet behind?" He gave a brittle laugh, shaking his head. He didn't know why it surprised him. After all, she'd been gone for six months when Violet was only a year old, returning only for the odd weekend. And again when she turned two.

"My job is important to me," she said tightly.

"When do you leave?" he asked.

"Tomorrow afternoon." Her eyes never strayed from his, but he thought he detected a hint of regret in her gaze.

"Does Violet know yet?" he asked.

Dana shook her head. "Not yet. I thought we could tell her together. It might make it easier."

"For who? You?" Ben cursed under his breath. It was always this game between them. Dana was good cop, he was bad cop. He was tired of cleaning up her mess. "Fine," he ground out. "But only for Violet. I want her to know she's safe. Secure." *That I won't be running off on her, too*, he thought. "Maybe it would be easier for her if I moved back in while you're away."

Dana bit her lip. "About that. Given the uncertainty, I've decided to put the house on the market."

Ben felt his jaw slack. "You *what*?"

"I've been thinking about it anyway," Dana said, crossing her arms defensively across her chest. "It's a big house. Too big for two people."

She was right about that. It was built for a family. And they were hardly a family anymore, were they?

He looked around the room, at the white cabinets they'd selected together, the arched window above the sink where they could watch Violet play on her swing set.

"I'm sorry, Ben," Dana said. "I know how much this house meant to you."

He nodded curtly. "It did mean a lot." But not for the reasons she thought. Sure, he'd overseen the plan, Sullivan Construction had done the labor, but the real reason he'd loved this house was because of what it represented. He closed his eyes for a moment. "It's probably time to let it go."

Dana motioned to Violet with her eyes. "So do you think we should tell her?"

"Now's as good a time as any," Ben said, hating the

heaviness that had settled over his chest. For the second time in two years they were going to sit down together and break their little girl's heart. And for the second time, it wasn't of his choosing.

But this would be the last time, he vowed to himself. So help him, from here on out he would make sure that his daughter's life was stable and secure and that no one would come along and turn their worlds upside down again.

# Chapter Three

At three o'clock sharp the next afternoon, Ben stood outside the brick building where Violet attended kindergarten. He'd rescheduled his meetings and taken the day off from work, using it instead to move as much of Violet's belongings as she might need into her smaller bedroom in his apartment. When he'd told Dana his lawyer would be in touch with hers to formally revisit their custody agreement, all she had done was nod. There was no use in fighting it, he supposed. She'd made her decision, weighed it, and understood the consequences. But had she taken Violet's feelings into account at all? He wanted to think so, but he was too angry to think clearly.

Realizing he was gritting his teeth, Ben tried to loosen his jaw before the bell rang and the kids poured from the front door of the school. He didn't want Violet to see him agitated or upset. He wanted her to think that all of this was somehow okay. Even though it wasn't.

He spotted her the moment the doors opened, her little red coat buttoned up to the neck, her ponytail coming undone, her eyes darting back and forth over the crowd of parents gathered outside the gate.

He hated to think that she was looking for a person who wasn't there, and wouldn't be again for a long time, if his hunch was correct. He plastered a smile on his face, and waved until he caught her attention, but her smile dropped as she approached him. "Fran usually picks me up," she informed him as a little line appeared between her eyebrows.

Ben didn't have the heart to tell her that her nanny was going to be working with another family now, and that she'd be going to the school's aftercare program starting next week instead. According to Dana, Fran was in great demand, and Fran didn't like the idea of hanging out in a bachelor pad all day.

"I thought it might be fun to spend some special time together this afternoon. Just you and me, what do you say?"

Violet considered this. "But it's not Wednesday."

*Or every other Saturday*, he thought, feeling the frustration mount in his chest. That's what his role as a parent had been limited to. Well, not anymore. He wasn't the one bailing, skipping town, flying off across the world when opportunity struck. He was here. Then. Now.

Always.

"Nope," he said, taking her by the hand and leading her to the car, careful to sidestep the icy puddles of slush. "That's what makes it special."

"But what about Mommy?" Violet asked, her voice pitching, a sign that she was on the brink of tears.

Ben stopped walking. He squeezed his free hand into a fist. He should have known the conversation last night wouldn't be the end of it. The tears she'd shed over the news had nearly torn his heart out, and he couldn't even look at Dana while they discussed the new arrangement with their daughter. In the end, they'd painted a brighter picture than it was, hoping they could live up to the rosy image.

"Remember, honey, Mommy had to take a business trip."

Violet's lower lip began to tremble. Ben bit back a sigh and crouched to wrap his arms around his child. She still seemed so small, and even though she loved to brag that she was a big girl, in kindergarten now, he couldn't resist. He picked her up, holding her close against his chest until her tears had turned to sniffles, and carried her on his hip the entire two blocks back to the car, remembering why he hated driving in the city.

Once they had climbed over the snowbanks and were settled in the car, he turned on the radio, even let Violet choose the song. He thought they were over the hump until Violet informed him they were going the wrong way.

"You're coming back to the apartment," he said

lightly. He eyed her in the rearview mirror. Her eyes were still watery, and he could tell by the pinch of her brow that she was on the verge of tears again.

"But my toys! I need my bunny!"

Ben was overjoyed to be presented with a problem he could actually solve. "But I have your bunny! She's at home, on your bed, waiting for you."

There was a pause as this sunk in. "But what about my clothes? And my hair bows?"

"All at the apartment," he said with forced cheer.

"But . . . what about my furniture?"

Ben blew out a sigh. "That's at the other house, Violet. Remember you have a bed and dresser at the apartment. And the pretty purple bedspread you chose?"

Violet grumbled something and leaned her head back against her car seat. She didn't say anything more until they pulled up in front of the building.

"Would you look at that?" Ben exclaimed. "A spot right in front. Must be our lucky day." He turned to catch Violet's eye but she just stared listlessly out the window.

Clenching his jaw, Ben pushed open his door and went around the car to help Violet undo her buckle. "Hey, I have an idea. We can have a pizza party tonight. How does that sound?"

He waited for the entire walk to the door for Violet to reply, but she didn't. Slowly, they trudged up the stairs. The building was quiet. No sounds came from the unit across the hall. Ben thought of the package Mary had given him and felt his spirits lift. He'd been saving it for Violet's birthday, but maybe he'd give it to her early as a little surprise.

His hand suddenly stilled with realization. Violet's birthday. It was only a week and a half away and her mother wouldn't be here to spend it with her. He frowned, looking down at the quiet little girl.

"So what do you say?" he asked again, as he took her small owl-shaped backpack and hooked it on the doorknob. "Should we order a pizza later? I'll even swing for extra cheese."

But Violet just walked past him and into the small room he'd made up for her when Dana had turned their lives upside down for the first time.

Ben stared at the hallway, racking his mind for what to do, how to make this better. But there was nothing he could do, he knew. Other than wait. And hope.

*

When things got rough, there was only one thing to do, and that was to take action! Mary had never been one to sit back and do nothing, to let the fates decide her future, to roll along with the punches. Nope, if she'd done that, then Sunshine Creamery would have never reopened again, and she would have still been working in that boring doctor's office, answering phones, and dodging little winks and glances from her middle-aged boss on his way to the water fountain.

So, yes, today had been a bad day. A very bad day

indeed. Nearly as bad as yesterday. But she needed to look at the bright side. Yes, she had a busted pipe, and yes, every single plumber that had stopped by had discovered even bigger problems as they investigated her situation, and yes, it would seem that things weren't exactly up to "code" and that she might have known this had she done a full renovation of the shop instead of a cosmetic face-lift, and that yes, this was all going to cost a small fortune. Far more than she could afford. But the bright side was that, for now, the water was back on at least. Even if she had just all but maxed out her credit card in the process. And even if it did seem that more problems were imminent.

Mary sunk her face into her hands and closed her eyes, indulging in a brief, but deep, moment of what she might describe as extreme self-pity, and then just as quickly, fluffed her hair and squared her shoulders.

She had learned over time that the best way to handle overwhelming problems like this was to break them down into palatable, bite-sized chunks. The first chunk: not enough money. How to solve that? Earn more, of course! And since it didn't seem like anyone wanted to buy her ice cream these days, she could only hope they might want to buy some of the old, well, treasures, she had stored up in this apartment.

Mary held out her sign and smiled at it with satisfaction. Yes, a building yard sale would be just the trick. If they all pulled together, they could attract quite a

crowd, and if she sold enough, then she'd at least be able
to cover the cost of the latest repairs. The rest, she hoped,
could be put off until after the weather turned warmer
and her business traffic picked up.

Mary pushed back her kitchen chair and grabbed her
roll of tape from the top drawer. The needling thought
that a yard sale in the snow might not exactly yield the
kind of results she wanted continued to worry her, but
then she thought, maybe someone had a heat lamp. Or
they could put out some fire pits, maybe even sell some
s'mores. Yes, s'mores. Now that would get people curious
for sure!

Feeling better, Mary opened her front door, her
shoulders squared with determination, and came face to
face with none other than Ben. Handsome, scowling Ben.

"Oh," she said, a little surprised. "Hello."

Ben shifted his dark blue eyes to the right, as if
contemplating darting back behind his door. "Hey," he
muttered, running a hand through his dark brown hair in
obvious agitation.

Mary pressed her lips together. So he was back to
wanting to ignore her. She could play that game, if he was
so insistent. Still, it seemed rude to just walk past him, like
they hadn't chatted last night, like he didn't live right
across the hall, with some woman named Violet . . .

Right. No use lingering on that chiseled jaw and that
deep-set gaze a second longer. So one of the best-looking
men she'd come across in a while happened to live right
across the hall. The man was taken. And he was also,

from what she could tell, a complete jerk.

And hadn't she had enough of those? She could almost see Jason's eye roll now. If he wasn't supportive back when Sunshine Creamery was doing well, she could only imagine what he'd have to say now.

Doubt caused her to worry her lip. Maybe he had been on to something. Maybe he'd been right. Maybe she'd been a fool to think she could turn the family business around. Maybe if she'd still been answering phones at the doctor's office, Jason wouldn't have dumped her. Via text.

Mary gripped her roll of tape a little tighter in her hand, and moved toward the stairs at the same moment at Ben. "Oh," she said, startling.

"Sorry." Ben frowned, and stepped back just when she did.

Mary's arm brushed his, and she quickly moved to the left, but again, there he was, and she laughed under her breath as his tall, hard body skimmed hers. He was wearing cologne, or maybe it was just soap—a faint, musky, manly scent. She hadn't realized just how tall he was before. At least six feet, and broad in the shoulders. Her eyes drifted over the curve of his biceps under his rugby shirt, until she felt the heat of his stare on hers. He didn't look amused. She laughed again, and stepped back properly this time. "Go ahead."

"Ladies first," he said tightly.

Geez, would it kill the man to smile? Mary felt her own

grin leave her face. He really was nothing short of unfriendly. Really, would it hurt him to have a little chitchat? It didn't have to mean anything. She was his neighbor, for God's sake. Was it too much to expect a simple wave and a smile every now and again, or maybe even someone willing to sign for the occasional package or water a plant?

From the set of his jaw and the steel in his eyes, she decided that yes, this was too much. Pity.

Mary skipped down the stairs, her hand light on the banister, aware of his heavy tread behind her as she wound her way down to the first floor and into the small vestibule where the mailboxes lined the wall. Ben brushed by her, as if she was a stranger in the building, not his next-door neighbor, not someone she'd done a recent favor for, and opened the front door.

Mary watched the exchange with the delivery man through the corner of her eye as she removed her recycling program sign from the glass door to the stairwell. Pizza. No surprise there. She'd smelled the pepperoni and cheese wafting through the hall night after night since moving in. Each time her stomach rumbled, sometimes tempting her to order one of her own. But then she would remember how slow business was these days, and how even little indulgences were an extravagance at the moment, and then she'd go pour a bowl of cereal or something equally depressing.

Mary shivered as a cold blast of air cut through the small lobby area, slicing through her angora sweater. She hurried to cut the tape, eager to get on her way before Ben had something snide to say about her "little initiative." If he bothered to say anything to her at all.

The front door closed, and all at once the room became warmer. Mary felt her skin heat, and her neck and cheeks flush as she sensed Ben standing behind her, and she knew it had nothing to do with the steam crackling from the ancient radiator in the corner.

"Almost finished," she said, not turning around. She smacked the last piece of tape against the bottom corner of the paper, annoyed to see that it bent slightly in her rush, and said briskly over her shoulder, "There. All done."

Ben glanced at her and then, without a word, leaned over her shoulder to inspect her handiwork. Mary felt her breath catch at his proximity, at the strange intimacy of the moment. She suddenly felt conspicuous and all too aware that they were alone in this small, cramped room, that her cheeks were warm and her heart was beating a little faster than usual, and that there was a telltale glint in Ben's eyes.

She should have added that footnote, excluding him from participation.

"A yard sale." He cocked an eyebrow at her, pulling back. "You do know it's March, don't you?"

"The start of spring," she said brightly, even though his pessimistic reminder had made her heart sink a little. "Most people do spring cleaning around this time of year.

It seems like the perfect opportunity to host a building yard sale."

His gaze was unwavering. Mary shifted on her feet. He was making her nervous. She suddenly wished he would go back to not talking to her at all. It was far easier than being forced to look up at those unreadable eyes, that nut brown hair that tousled this way and that, and those smooth, pink lips that were curved . . . into a bit of a smirk, she realized.

She rolled her shoulders. Well. Time to come to her senses.

"Have you been outside lately?" he asked in a pleasant enough tone.

"Yes, I have obviously been outside," she said hastily. She reached for the door handle and tugged it a few times, until she remembered that it swung open, instead. Her cheeks were on fire as she briefly met Ben's questioning gaze from the corner of her eye, his smirk now a wicked grin.

"I think you have to push it." Ben's voice was low and deep in her ear, with a hint of amusement.

Mary huffed, feeling her face grow hot. "I know that." She pushed it open and began walking up the stairs, trying her best not to think about the fact that Ben had a perfect view of her butt for the entire walk back to the third floor.

She fought the urge to stop walking, to say she'd forgotten something downstairs, needed to check her mail, something, anything, that would get him away from her, and from the close proximity of her backside. At the next landing, she slanted him a glance, but his eyes were focused on the pizza box, and the little frown was back, pulling at his features.

Mary frowned with him, suddenly a little insulted to realize he hadn't taken the opportunity to check her out. He was a man after all, and even if there was someone named Violet in his life, most hot-blooded males of a certain age would still take a moment to sneak a peek.

He was clearly very loyal to this Violet woman. Mary couldn't help the stab of jealousy that panged. It would be nice to find a man like that, wouldn't it?

Except that she wasn't looking for a man. Not now. Not with everything else going on. Not after the last guy had so neatly stomped on her heart.

Finally, they were at their landing. Mary had left her door unlocked, and she was now grateful for it. She could slip inside, close the door, beat him at his own game. Except that wasn't like her, was it?

"Well, good night." She smiled as she wrapped her hand around the brass doorknob and paused.

Ben skirted her a glance as he balanced the pizza box in one hand and reached into his pocket to fetch his key with his other. "Mmm," he simply muttered, and turned his back to stick the key into its slot.

Mary stared at his back. His strong, broad, perfectly attractive back, if there were even such a thing, which she now knew with certainty there was, and scowled. Enough was enough. She'd gone out of her way, shown a little bit of kindness, and time after time the man was hell-bent on giving her the cold shoulder.

She pushed open the door of her apartment and closed it without another word. But she couldn't resist one more glance through the peephole. After all, the man might be a jerk, but there was certainly no harm in looking.

# Chapter Four

Any hopes Ben had of a peaceful weekend family breakfast were already shattered, and it wasn't even half past seven.

"They're supposed to be yellow on the inside," Violet insisted, "not all mashed up. I don't like them like this!"

Ben plucked two pieces of rye bread from the toaster and stood at the counter, trying to keep the impatience from creeping into his voice. In the few short days since Dana had left town and Violet had moved in, he'd sensed a shift in his daughter. She used to look forward to her visits with him, even if he'd hated that word—visits—as if he were a distant relative or something. "They're eggs, Violet, how bad could they be?"

"They're not sunny eggs! I like sunny eggs."

"They're scrambled, not sunny side-up," he muttered

under his breath and grabbed the coffee pot, sloshing the contents as he refilled his mug. Cursing, he mopped the mess with a rag, and turned to Violet in exasperation. "This is all you're getting until lunch, so please just eat it."

"Mommy makes me sunny eggs."

She had to keep hitting that nerve. "Well," he replied as he set his plate on the table with a clatter, "your mother isn't here, I am."

Instantly, tears welled in Violet's eyes and Ben brought his hand to his forehead. "Oh God. Violet, honey, I'm sorry. I just . . . I'm trying, Violet. I just . . . What about the toast?"

Violet pushed her plate away and Ben dragged out a sigh. It was going to be another one of those days, and this time there wasn't an office to run to, or the hope that a few hours at school, in her usual daily routine, with her friends, would shake Violet out of her funk. The kid missed her mom, and despite his feelings for Dana at this point, he couldn't blame her.

Leaning against the counter, Ben picked up his fork, his appetite now gone, and cut into his eggs. One bite confirmed Violet's accusations. Cold. Rubbery. Overcooked. Dana's eggs were always timed to perfection. Who could blame the kid for not eating?

He should have stuck with the frozen waffles. The kind she ate every other time she spent the night here. Instead he'd tried to do something special. He set his plate in the sink, reaching instead for his mug of coffee. He eyed Violet over the rim, his chest tightening at the sight.

Her cheek was cupped in her hand, her eyes downcast, her lower lip jutting slightly. Ben closed his eyes, swallowing hard, and took another sip of the coffee, the one thing he knew how to make properly—if making coffee even classified as cooking. He had a feeling Violet would tell him it didn't. He leaned back against the counter, letting his gaze fall over the adjacent living room. He'd lived here for two years and there still weren't any pictures on the walls. It would have made it feel too permanent, but now he realized his error. If Violet was going to be staying with him going forward, he'd need a new place. And until then, he needed to spruce this one up.

"How about we go shopping today? I could use your help decorating your room a bit more."

Violet eyed him uncertainly. "I have a room. At my house."

Ben gripped the mug tighter. The house no longer belonged to him, and he wasn't involved in the selling process, but he knew Chicago real estate, and he knew the quality of the house's construction. He wouldn't be surprised if it already had an offer.

He grimaced, trying not to think of all the hope and possibility that house had once held. That it would now belong to another family. That he'd failed somehow. And that his daughter was paying the price.

*

Mary scraped the last of the batter into the waffle cone press and sighed. She'd been hoping the snow would let up by now, but it was colder this morning than it had been in days, and the snow that had fallen earlier in the week still stubbornly stuck to the bushes and hugged the curbs in high piles.

She glanced out the window forlornly, only looking up when she'd realized she'd burned the last of the waffle cones by taking her eye off it too long. No bother, she thought, tossing it in the trash. It wasn't as if she were likely to sell out today. Not with the wind howling that way . . .

She pressed a fist against her apron and turned back to the counter. Normally she would be preparing a fresh flavor of the day, or dreaming up new ones for tomorrow, but she was tired, and her heart was heavy, and—oh, crap—her sister was at the door.

Scrambling to adjust her expression into something more cheerful, she hurried to the door and turned the locks. Lila shivered as she stepped inside the shop and rubbed her mitten-covered hands together. "It's freezing out there!"

Mary felt her lips thin. So she'd noticed on her walk into work this morning. It had taken everything in her not to turn around, go back to bed, and stay there until spring.

"To what do I owe the honor?" she asked. Her voice felt tight and her pulse was speeding up. Had Lila noticed

the lack of traffic? Was she concerned? It wasn't often
that she swung by unannounced like this.

"Oh, Sam went to the gym and I'm on my way to a
stationary shop down the street. I thought I'd stop by and
get your thoughts on the wedding invitations. Unless this
is a bad time?" Her large grey eyes swept the empty room.

"Not a bad time at all," Mary insisted. "I don't open
for another hour, so you beat the rush." The rush! She all
but snorted, but managed to stop herself just in time.

Lila didn't seem to notice as she sat down on a counter
stool and unraveled her scarf. "Got any coffee hiding
back there?" she asked, lifting her chin to the back room
where she knew Mary kept a percolator. "Actually, I can
see you're busy, so I'll go make us some."

She started to get off the stool, but Mary sprung
forward, stopping her. "No. No, you sit," she said shakily,
ignoring Lila's quizzical expression. "I have some already
made. I'll . . . be right back."

She hurried to the back of the shop and let herself into
the room. Most of the evidence from the broken pipe had
been cleaned up by now, with the exception of the glaring
hole in the ceiling where the drywall had been ripped out.
She eyed the piles of receipts and bills that littered the
small desk in the corner, and then closed her eyes for a
beat. She took three deep breaths, trying to calm herself.
The pipes weren't going to burst again—at least she
hoped they weren't—but something did need to be done.
And it probably didn't just stop with the plumbing.

All she needed now was a surprise inspection. Wouldn't that just be the cherry on top of her sundae?

This shop had been in her grandparents' possession for as long as she'd known them. Longer than she'd been alive. Sunshine Creamery was a neighborhood institution, a throwback to the sweeter days, and, she was starting to realize, a money pit.

"Need help back there?" Lila called from the storefront.

Stiffening, Mary grabbed two mugs and sloshed some coffee into them. "Nope, all set!"

She managed to smile serenely as she carried the coffees back to her sister. "I couldn't find the sugar," she explained.

Lila narrowed her gaze. "This is an ice cream parlor. Don't you have pounds of sugar?"

Mary felt her cheeks flush as she took the stool next to her sister. She wasn't thinking clearly, and her behavior was starting to reflect it. "Oh. I didn't feel like opening a new bag. Anyway . . . How's Sam?"

As suspected, Lila was immediately distracted. They chatted about her upcoming wedding plans, her thoughts on the dress, and the flowers, the invitations of course, and then, as they always did, they talked about Gramps.

"I know it might have been unrealistic, but I always thought he'd be here to walk us down the aisle," Lila said wistfully.

Mary swallowed the knot in her throat. "I know. I always thought so, too." She stared at the framed photo she'd hung on the wall of the man who had raised them, standing behind this very counter, grinning ear to ear. He'd kept this place running for how many years, and she was in risk of losing it in a matter of months. How was that even possible?

She looked away. She loved having this photo here, with her all day, but sometimes . . . well, sometimes it just plain hurt. She remembered when she was little, and she and Lila had just moved in with their grandparents, how much it hurt to see the pictures of her parents, to know that they were gone and never coming back. In time that pain had faded. She wasn't so sure how she felt about the pain fading again.

Every time she pushed through the door of Sunshine Creamery, it was as if Gramps was here with her. As if she still had a home base, a piece of her past, of her childhood.

She glanced at her sister. She had Lila. At least she had her.

"Although," Mary said, taking a sip of her coffee and bringing herself back to the conversation. "I guess it was never in the cards for Gramps to walk me down an aisle. I doubt I'll ever get married."

"What?" Lila laughed. "Please. You're just in a rut. You'll find someone."

"I'm not so sure," Mary admitted truthfully. She hardly got out much, and it wasn't like the man she was going to marry was just going to come along and knock on her door.

She frowned, thinking of Ben across the hall, and set down her mug with a thud.

"It's not like you to sound so defeated," Lila remarked. She studied Mary's face with concern. "Is everything okay?"

Mary shifted uneasily on her seat. She used to tell her sister everything. Even though she was only a couple years older, Lila had always been more levelheaded and mature, forced to grow up a little sooner when their parents had died. She'd always been protective of Mary, always there to offer her support. Lila would give Mary the shirt off her back, and she almost had, considering the money she'd given to revive Sunshine Creamery, all because Mary couldn't bring herself to let it go.

She knew that if she told Lila about the plumbing problems, and possibly some electrical wiring issues too, not to mention that gaping hole in the ceiling, that her sister would heave a sigh and do what she could. But Mary wasn't ten years old anymore. And her sister had done enough. She was planning a wedding. Starting a new advertising agency. Mary wasn't that selfish.

No, this was her problem to solve. And she would solve it. Somehow.

*

Ben looked down at Violet's small hand in his and squeezed it a little tighter. Determined to keep his tone light, he said, "Are you hungry?"

She hadn't eaten the eggs he'd made, and by now several hours had passed. He looked around at his options, eyeing a bagel shop just ahead. "How about a bagel?"

But even though they were her favorite, Violet just shook her head. "When's Mommy coming back?" she asked again.

Ben pulled in a breath and put one foot in front of the other. He'd answered this question over and over, but it didn't seem any of his responses were good enough. And there was a possibility they never would be.

Dana had always traveled for her job—it was a sticking point earlier in their marriage, when Violet was first born, and it had stayed that way right up until the bitter end. *And beyond*, he thought. Usually Violet was oblivious to her absence, knowing she would be back on a set day, usually full of souvenirs. That had been a sticking point, too.

But things were different now, and Violet was old enough to sense it. This wasn't just a night or two with Daddy; this was new territory. He could only hope they fell into a new routine soon. And that Dana didn't come along and shake it up all over again.

"What about a burger?" he said, pointing to a restaurant. "I'll let you have some fries."

But Violet shook her head again. Exasperated, Ben stopped walking and crouched down until he was eye to eye with his daughter. The little pout of her mouth tore at his heart.

"Listen, Violet, I know you're confused, and I know you miss your mother, but I'm trying, honey. I'm trying to do something nice for you. So if you won't eat what I'm offering, then is there anything else you might want?"

He waited a beat, about to give up, when Violet said in a soft voice, "Maybe some ice cream."

Ben almost pointed out that it was below freezing and the wind was picking up, but then thought the better of it. The kid wanted ice cream. And ice cream she would have.

"I seem to recall seeing a place around here," he said, leading her by the hand. They hurried another block, until the familiar sign with the drawing of the sun came into view. Ben grinned. Finally, something was going right today.

His tread was lighter all the way to the front door, until he glanced through the window and saw nothing but empty chairs and tables. An old jukebox in the back corner. He tried the door, relieved to find it moved, that he wouldn't need to let his daughter down yet again, no matter how small the way.

No one was behind the counter, and for a moment Ben wondered if the place really was open for business. He glanced at Violet, whose doleful eyes spoke his same sentiment, and chewed the inside of his lip, quickly weighing his options.

He was just about to give up when he heard a rustling of feet from the hall at the back of the room. He frowned as a woman came into view. It couldn't be . . . Not . . .

"Mary?"

Her eyes widened ever so slightly in surprise, and her cheeks grew pink. "Ben." She walked toward them, her hips swaying in those tight jeans, her forehead pinching for one telling second as she dropped her gaze to Violet. Looking back to him, she said, "What brings you here?"

He tipped his head. The confusion in this instance was mutual. "Do you work here?"

Mary grinned. "I own it, actually."

"It suits you," he said, meaning it. He swept his eyes around the place, taking in the small tables that dotted the room, the pastel-hued palette, the modern touches in an otherwise old facility.

She seemed pleased to hear it. "Thanks. I think so too."

His gaze roamed quickly over her soft camel sweater that scooped just low enough to reveal a smooth collarbone and the hint of something beyond. "Perhaps you can help us, then." He noticed the way her brow furrowed on the word "us."

"What can I do for you?" She tipped her head, locking her eyes with his, and he had the urge to look away, to not get sucked into her friendly disposition, her patient gaze, her small smile.

"It seems we're in need of some ice cream," he said, winking at Violet and giving her hand a little shake.

Finally, Mary turned her attention from him, and smiled warmly at his daughter. "Well, then, you've come to the right place." She lifted her arm to the chalkboard sign above the counter. "Any flavor you'd like. And I even have sprinkles," she added, smiling at Violet.

Ben studied the impressive list. Cherry cheesecake. Peaches and cream. Certainly not your run of the mill flavors. He slanted Mary a glance, feeling her watching him. "Do you make the ice cream yourself?"

"That I do," she said. She dropped her attention to Violet. "In fact, I was about to make a fresh batch of raspberry white-chocolate chip. If you're not in a hurry, you can help me." She looked up at Ben for permission.

Ben rolled back on his heels, thinking of an excuse to be on his way, back to the apartment, where he and Violet could do their own thing, mind their own business, but then he caught the hopeful look in his daughter's eyes. One he hadn't seen since Dana had delivered the news the other night at the house.

"That sounds like a real treat," he said.

"I'm Mary, by the way," Mary said to Violet.

"This is my daughter," Ben offered. "Violet."

Mary's eyes widened ever so slightly. "I see. What a lovely name! I bet your favorite color is purple."

Violet's eyes lit up, and she nodded her head, beaming. "How'd you know that?"

Mary tossed Ben a wink. "Lucky guess."

"Well, Violet, the first thing you need to do is cover your pretty outfit with an apron." She helped Violet out of her coat and then tied a cotton apron around her waist, careful to fold it over at the waist so it didn't skim the floor. Violet giggled with delight as Mary led her behind the counter. She cocked an eyebrow in Ben's direction. "You're welcome to join in."

"No, thanks," he said, holding up his hands. "I'm happy to watch." And he was. Happy to see the light return to his daughter's eyes, the smile to her face.

He settled onto a stool and let his gaze wander over the room as Mary measured ingredients and helped Violet pour them into a bowl. "This is a nice place," he mused. "How'd you come to own it?"

"Family business," Mary explained, as she brought out a plastic container of oversized chocolate chips.

So that explained the ice cream social. It didn't, however, explain all her other building initiatives. "You must keep busy," he remarked, wondering how she found the time to bother with things like community yard sales.

"Oh." Mary picked up a wooden spoon and began stirring some raspberries into a creamy concoction. "Yes, this store is my top priority, you might say."

Ben wondered why he felt so disappointed. Sure she was pretty, but she was also annoying as hell with all her peppy signs and cheerful ideas. But it wasn't like he was interested in her. He wasn't interested in anyone. Especially another woman who made their job their top priority.

He frowned, thinking of Violet's mother. She'd said she would try to call today. For Violet's sake, he hoped she stuck to that promise.

"I hope you like raspberries," Mary was saying now.

"They're my mommy's favorite fruit," Violet said, and Ben's pulse kicked with panic. Everything was going so well, and now . . . He held his breath, waiting for the fallout. "It's too bad she isn't here to enjoy them."

Mary's brow creased slightly. "Oh. Well, you can bring her some of this ice cream if you'd like," she suggested.

"No." Violet shook her head and stared at the ground. "She went away for a while. I'm living with Daddy now."

Ben balled a fist at his side, waiting for the tears. Wishing there was something he could do. But all he could do was sit and watch. And wait. Mary met his eye and gave a sad smile. Ben swallowed hard, locking her gaze with his, feeling their warmth across the room.

"I see," Mary said. "Well, when I'm feeling a little sad, do you know what always cheers me up?" She bent down and stage-whispered into Violet's ear, "Ice cream!"

Violet's eyes danced and she began to laugh. "Me too!"

"Then should we turn this into ice cream?" Mary asked, taking the bowl to a machine. Ben's chest tightened at the ease with which she did this. Soon, Violet was laughing along with Mary, excitedly asking questions about the process, as if the earlier setback had never even happened. He had the urge to stand up and join in, but he stopped himself.

He held back, not wanting to ruin this, not wanting to interfere.

This was a step. One step at a time.

After the ice cream mixture was all in the machine,

Mary made Violet her requested banana split and then turned to Ben. "Let me guess, lemon sorbet."

Ben frowned. "How'd you guess?"

"Oh." Mary's pretty lips twisted into a pert little smile as she reached for a metal scooper. "It's this little game I play. I like to guess which flavor people will choose. Most of the time I'm right, too."

"And you guessed lemon sorbet for me because . . ." He tipped his head in question and met Mary's knowing gaze. Of course. Because he was a little sour. Instead of feeling the brush of insult, he tipped back his head and laughed. The sound was unfamiliar, distant, like a part of himself that had gotten lost somewhere along the way. And maybe it had. "Okay, you got me. But we can't all be as friendly as you." He picked up his spoon as Mary slid a ruffle-edged glass bowl across the counter. The color was soft yellow, the texture creamy to the eye, and despite the fact that he would really prefer a hot cup of coffee to a cold bowl of sorbet, he brought a scoop to his mouth.

"This is really good," he said, eagerly dipping his spoon in again.

"You sound surprised," Mary said, a hint of amusement in her tone as she leaned a hip into the counter. He caught her smile, the hint of the mirth in her big brown eyes, the way a few wisps of her auburn hair had come free of the ponytail that showed off her long, slender neck.

He swallowed the bite, looked down at his bowl. "I'm

just surprised there isn't a line out the door," he said.

"Have you been outside lately?" she asked, repeating the very question he'd asked of her the other night. A mischievous smile danced through her eyes, but her smile seemed to slip.

"Touché," he said, grinning.

"Winter is my slow season," Mary sighed. "Other than a few birthday parties here and there, it's just a trickle of customers throughout the day. It's quiet, but I don't mind so much."

"Well, spring should be here in no time."

She nodded firmly. "It should. But between you and me, I'm struggling to believe that." She laughed, a light and airy sound that floated through the room, and then looked over at Violet, who was busy scraping the last of the whipped cream from her bowl. She smiled at what she saw, seeming nearly as satisfied with the visit as Ben. "Ice cream. Does the trick every time."

"I'll remember that," Ben said, even though he hoped there wouldn't be a next time. Maybe today's outing had forced Violet from her bad mood at last. Maybe they could have a nice weekend together and then resume their new routine next week.

Or maybe the second they left here, she'd go back to being sullen and quiet.

His chest tightened as he opened his wallet and handed over a twenty, but his frown relaxed when his fingers brushed Mary's, and a burst of electricity shot up his arm. He watched as she tucked a strand of auburn hair behind her ear and rang up his purchase, chatting happily with Violet, who was kneeling on her stool to study all the ice cream flavors in the glass case below.

"I guess I'll see you around the building then," he said. His voice felt thick and foreign, as if it didn't belong to his own body.

Mary did a good job of concealing her own surprise, and Ben held his breath, wondering how she'd reply, if she'd say something snippy or sarcastic. God knew he deserved it. His hand still held the memory of her touch, and he suddenly realized he hoped to see her around the building. And soon.

# Chapter Five

Well, one mystery was solved. Violet was not Ben's wife, but rather, his completely adorable daughter. Mary tried to wrap her head around this information as she maneuvered her way over a snowbank on her way to Corner Beanery, where she was meeting Lila for Monday morning coffee, a new ritual in their lives since they no longer spent every weekend together as they did when they were roommates. She huddled against the cold, the wind almost taunting her, reminding her of her circumstances, and then she cursed as a cab swerved to a stop and splashed icy cold water against her coat.

So much for saving a few bucks by walking.

Lila was stepping out of a cab as Mary approached the coffee shop. Her sister looked fresh faced and put together. No traces of dirty water all over her winter white coat, Mary observed, looking down at her own black down parka.

"Hailey said her cousin was stopping by today," Lila said, as she pulled open the door. She paused, and gave Mary the once-over. "Did you walk all the way here?"

"It's not so far," Mary said, but they both knew that wasn't true. "And I needed the exercise."

"I won't ask you again about joining my gym," Lila said with a smile.

Mary's own expression was a little shaky as they stomped the snow from their boots on the mat in the vestibule. "You know the gym is expensive," she said. It was the most she ever expressed about her budget; at first she hoped it relayed to Lila that she was being frugal, being wise with her money, but now she wondered if her sister saw something more in the statement.

From the casual shrug she gave before turning to look for Hailey, it didn't seem so.

Hailey was foaming milk, chatting with a pretty blond-haired girl perched on a stool beside the espresso machine. "Girls, this is my cousin Claire."

"Hailey mentioned you were staying with her for a while," Lila said as they took their seats beside her.

"Hopefully not for long," Claire said with a cheeky smile. She glanced at her cousin. "No offense."

"None taken!" Hailey exclaimed as she poured the frothy milk into a mug. "It will be nice to see the floor again. I've almost forgotten what color it is!"

Claire blushed. "I was supposed to be moving across country," she explained to Mary and Lila. "Instead, all of my belongings have ended up in Hailey's one-bedroom apartment."

"There might be some openings in my building," Mary offered, and her mind again wandered back to Ben. He'd seemed different the other day at Sunshine Creamery. Softer. Maybe it was because he had his daughter with him, she mused. She definitely brought out his sweeter side.

"Thanks, but I first have to get a job," Claire said. "I gave up the last one when I thought I was moving, and helping out here for a few hours a week isn't going to cut it."

Hailey was shaking her head, her mouth pinched in disapproval. "When I think of what that guy did to you."

Claire just waved a hand through the air and took a sip of her latte. "It's fine. Really. For the best." She slid Mary a wry smile. "Or so I tell myself."

"My last boyfriend dumped me on New Year's Eve," Mary confided. "How do you think that bodes for the rest of my year?" She grinned up at Hailey, who handed her a mug of her favorite coffee blend.

"I think it bodes very well!" Lila said firmly. "This year is a clean slate. The future is wide open."

Mary tipped her chin and leveled her sister with a long look. "You sound like me." Or how she once felt. It had been a while since she'd been that truly optimistic about anything. Sure, she tried to convince herself, tried to believe that everything would work out fine in the end, but more and more, she wasn't so sure.

She frowned. For a moment, she envied her sister's confidence. But then, her sister had a great job, a lovely apartment she could easily afford, and a handsome fiancé and a wedding on the horizon. Whereas Mary . . .

"You won't find love with that attitude," Lila scolded.

"Who said I was looking for love?" Mary replied.

"Well, why shouldn't you be?" Lila said. "You're young and pretty. Why let one bad experience spoil your future?"

But it wasn't just one bad experience. She rarely met anyone, and when she did, it never became serious. Jason was the closest thing to a real boyfriend she'd ever had. She'd cared about him, maybe even loved him, and she'd dreamed of a future together. And he'd ended it without a glance back. The thought of going through that again was too much to think about.

"I'm perfectly happy without a man in my life," Mary replied. "In fact, I'm happier. Now I can focus on Sunshine Creamery, and I don't have to worry about random text messages breaking my heart." She brought her mug to her lips and paused. "Did I mention he broke up with me via text?" she said to Claire.

One of Claire's fine eyebrows lifted. "Nice."

"Yeah," Mary said, pursing her lips. "Real nice."

"Jason was a jerk," Lila said airily. "You'll find someone else. You just have to be open to finding it.

And, you need to get out more."

"I'm out now!" Mary exclaimed. And yes, she did usually scan the coffee shop every time she entered, just in case. She wasn't completely closed off to love. She just wasn't exactly open to it.

"I keep saying it, but there are some cute guys at the gym . . ."

"Oh, there are!" Hailey agreed, nodding enthusiastically. "Not that I've had any luck with them. Still, it's not like you're going to stumble upon Mr. Right just next door. Your sister is right, Mary, you have to get out, go look for him."

Mary nodded thoughtfully, willing herself to stay quiet. Normally, she'd agree with Hailey, but after her last exchange with Ben, she couldn't help wondering if the tall, handsome, and completely elusive man wasn't just everything she'd been looking for all along.

If she was looking, that was.

*

Ben pulled the car to a stop in front of the school and flicked on his hazard lights. They were late. Again. Something he'd promised himself he wouldn't let happen. But then Violet had to burst into tears when he couldn't braid her hair the way Dana did, and then she'd refused to eat the pancakes he'd made her, even though they were in the shape of her initials.

He glanced at the clock on the dashboard, his jaw tensing. Ten minutes late today. His worst showing yet.

For a moment, he wondered if he could hack it. If he hadn't given his ex enough credit. If he'd overestimated his role as a father. But then he remembered that Dana was the one who had flown halfway across the world without much concern about when she'd return, and Ben was the one who, years after the divorce, still craved the family life he'd lost.

"Right, well, let's hurry," Ben said as he turned to face his daughter. Noticing her frown, he said, "Your birthday party is this weekend! I bet all the kids are excited."

"I don't want to have my party anymore," Violet muttered, and Ben stifled a sigh.

He was exasperated, tired, and frustrated as hell. He rubbed a hand over his face, refusing to let it show. "Aw, come on now. You'll have fun!"

"No I won't. Mommy made me have it at the bowling alley. I don't like bowling anymore." Her bottom lip began to quiver, and Ben clenched a fist at his side. Of course she didn't like bowling. It reminded her of her mother, just like it did for him. Back before the divorce, it was something they'd done together, especially on cold, winter weekends.

He thought fast. The invitations had been sent weeks ago; Dana had taken care of it all well before she'd left town. It wasn't exactly convenient to change plans now, but given the circumstances, he couldn't see another way. "We could have a pizza party instead," he offered. "Does that sound like fun?"

"Maybe we can have it at the ice cream place," Violet suggested, brightening. "The one with the nice lady!"

Ben frowned. He'd seen the way Violet responded to Mary, and while he appreciated it, was grateful for it, he didn't need to be making a habit of it. It was just . . . too complicated.

"Oh, I think she's probably very busy," Ben countered.

"No, she's not!" Violet cried. "There wasn't even anyone else in the shop!"

True, very true. Ben looked at his daughter. "We could have the party at that pizza place you like down in Bucktown. The one where you walk down the stairs—"

"But why can't we have it at the ice cream parlor?" Violet asked, her big blue eyes blinking in question.

Ben sighed. "I told you honey, it's short notice, and she's probably busy."

"Can you ask?" Violet asked, and Ben swallowed hard. It was a simple question. And it was her birthday. And as much as he wanted to, he couldn't think of a good enough reason to say no.

*

Four hours later, Ben tucked his head into his father's office. "I'm running out on an errand. Can I grab you anything for lunch while I'm out?"

His father shook his head. "Your mother has me on a diet." He scowled at the desk. "Salad. Soup. I'd kill for a burger."

Ben laughed. "I won't tell if you don't."

His father considered it for a moment. "No. She'd find out somehow. No doubt she'd smell it on my clothes."

Ben grinned. "And yet everyone worries that I miss married life . . . "

His father's expression turned into one that was all too familiar, the lines on his face etching in concern. "How are things going? With Violet?"

Ben leaned into the doorjamb. "She misses her mother. With her birthday this weekend, the timing couldn't be worse."

"Come up to the house," his father urged. "Let us do something special for her."

"She'd like that," Ben said. And he would, too. So long as his mother didn't try to set him up again.

Shrugging into his coat, he hurried down to the lobby of the office building and hailed a cab. According to Sunshine Creamery's website, it should be open by now, and he'd much prefer to have the conversation with Mary at her place of business rather than at the apartment building. Somehow knocking on her door felt too personal, it established a familiarity he wasn't comfortable with, upending the nice, big walls he'd made sure to put up when he first moved into the building.

The ice cream parlor looked just as empty today as it had over the weekend, Ben noticed when they pulled up to the corner twenty minutes later. He peered through the cab window, searching for the Open sign, and, only somewhat satisfied with his findings, paid the driver and climbed out.

The bell over the door jangled as he pushed it open, and Mary came all but running into the storefront at the sound, a huge smile on her face that slipped slightly when she saw him.

"Back again?" she remarked, recovering.

Ben shoved his hands into his pockets and rolled back on his heels. Her hair was astray, wisps shooting out from her forehead, and her cheeks were flushed, bringing out the brightness of her eyes. He allowed his gaze to drift lower, to the soft pull of her sweater over the swell of her breasts, and then yanked them back up, clearing his throat. There was no point in that. No point at all.

"I'm here on official business," he said.

"Oh?" She blinked in surprise, and if he didn't know better, he might say she'd gone a little pale.

"My daughter was quite impressed with your shop. She was hoping to have her birthday party here," he said, sliding her a smile.

"Of course!" Mary cried, in what Ben could only describe as relief. Her huge smile returned as she nodded enthusiastically. "I love doing children's parties. When is it?"

"This Saturday." He held up a hand before she could protest. "If it's too short of notice I completely understand if you're too busy." He glanced around the room, finding this possibility unlikely.

Mary stepped forward, and Ben fought the urge to step back. To put distance between himself and this pretty woman, this new force in his life, and, unsettlingly, his daughter's.

"It's not a problem at all," she said, reaching over the counter to grab a pad of paper and a pen. "What time did you have in mind?"

"I think the party starts at two," he said, bringing up a mental picture of the bowling invitation that had already been sent out.

"Two o'clock it is then!" Mary scribbled notes on her pad. "How many kids should I plan for?"

"I'll have to check on that. Ten or twelve, I think," Ben said.

"Perfect. They can build their own sundaes, and that old jukebox over there works if they like music. I loved dancing to that thing when I was a kid," she said wistfully.

Ben tipped his head, imagining Mary as a little girl Violet's age. She still had that youthful spark, that hope and energy that he'd somehow lost along the way. For a moment, he envied her for it.

"When you said this was a family business, I hadn't realized it went back that far."

Mary's eyes locked with his. "My grandparents opened it, long before my sister or I were born. I loved this place growing up. Still do." She gave a sad smile.

"Is that your grandfather?" Ben asked, motioning to the photo on the wall he'd seen during his last visit.

Mary nodded. "He passed away last year, so it's up to me to keep the place running now."

"That's a big undertaking," Ben remarked, sweeping his gaze over the room once more. He doubted traffic was always this slow. It was midweek and freezing cold outside, after all.

"Oh, you have no idea." Mary gave a low chuckle, a laugh that rumbled deep and steady, and Ben couldn't fight off his grin. He liked the sound of it. Wouldn't mind hearing it again. "I guess this building is old. My grandparents seemed to put most of their energy into making ice cream and keeping customers happy. They didn't pay much attention to the building itself, or things like electrical issues, plumbing issues." Her laugh turned a little shaky.

"Well, it's an old building, that's not uncommon," Ben said.

"No, I suppose not. But it seems that if I'm ever going to permanently solve some of these, well, issues, I'm having, then I need to do some maintenance before things progress."

Ben raised an eyebrow. He knew all about codes and inspection issues. Out of curiosity, he asked, "What is the issue exactly?"

"Oh, I had a frozen pipe that burst, and they switched out the pipe, for a small fortune of course," she added, pinching her lips. "But then they noticed the water heater probably won't last much longer, and . . . well, other things like that." She seemed to twitch.

Ben sucked in a breath. He'd heard enough. Mary was right; an old building was a big undertaking. Especially if you weren't prepared for it. He opened his mouth, a part of him wanting to offer his help, to look around, give her an honest opinion in case some less than reliable contractors had tried to take advantage, and then clamped his mouth shut. Mary was his neighbor. And he didn't need to be getting close. What he needed was to keep his distance, and remember that no good came from getting involved where he shouldn't.

"Anyway." Mary tapped her pen against her notepad. "Violet mentioned her favorite color was purple. Shall I go with that for the decorations? I can hang some balloons and streamers, and put out some matching tablecloths."

"That would be perfect," Ben said. He realized that Dana might have already coordinated everything with the bowling place, but like so many things in their lives since the divorce, he'd been left off the communication. "I've sort of been thrown into this at the last minute."

"Don't worry," Mary said, dismissing his concern. "We'll figure it out. Violet will have a wonderful party. I promise."

Ben frowned. He hadn't been a "we" in a long time, and the ease with which Mary said it seemed overly familiar, and almost . . . comforting. It brought him back to a more secure time and place, when he'd felt like part of a family, part of a team.

He eyed Mary cautiously, who seemed completely unaware of the impact of her last statement. Her smile was bright, her eyes so earnest, and her entire demeanor so self-assured, that he felt the tension begin to roll off his shoulders.

He had no doubt that Violet would have a wonderful party. And it was all thanks to Mary.

# Chapter Six

Mary finished hanging the last of the balloons and took a step back to admire her effort. Even with a critical eye, she had to say that she was impressed. Bunches of purple and pink balloons anchored each end of the counter, and in the center of the room, Mary had pushed the tables together to form a long, makeshift table, covered in a pretty lavender cloth. Bowls of colorful sprinkles, an assortment of chocolate chips, and even a selection of jelly beans were scattered along the party table, ready for the girls to make their ice cream sundaes. It was everything a little girl could want for a party. At least, she hoped so.

There was something about Violet, something that went a touch beyond shy, that made her worry. Mary fluffed up a paper pom-pom and did another quick sweep of the room. No use getting overly concerned. The little girl had a loving father. And there was obviously a mother in the picture, too. Somewhere.

The aprons were on the counter, and Mary began counting them out again, just to be sure she had enough, when the door jangled. Her heart did a little flip-flop, and she knew before she'd even looked up that it was Ben.

"Look at this place!" he exclaimed, and the grin on his face brought a smile to her own.

Mary looked down at Violet, who was wearing a purple dress and matching headband, her eyes huge as they took in the room. "Do you like it?" she dared to ask, and realized she was holding her breath as she waited for the response.

"This is way better than the bowling alley!" Violet cried, and Mary and Ben laughed.

"Let me take your coats," Mary said, helping Violet out of her down parka. She reached for Ben's coat, her fingers brushing with his instead of the soft wool. Sparks of heat shot through her belly, and she drew a sharp breath, breaking his stare. His coat felt heavy draped over her arm, soft but a little scratchy. A little like him, she mused. "I'll just go hang these up in the back room," she muttered, feeling the warmth spread to her cheeks.

Ridiculous! She gave herself a stern talking to all the way to the back room, where she hung each coat on the rack next to her own. Her fingers lingered on Ben's coat, the hint of musk coming off it. She pursed her lips, counted to three and told herself that enough was enough. The man was her neighbor. Her totally hot neighbor, but still her neighbor. And he was a father. And this was his child's birthday party. And the child's mother was probably about to come through the front door at any moment. And she was probably gorgeous. Surely she wouldn't miss her child's birthday!

Mary smoothed her ponytail and tapped her lips, making sure the gloss was still there. Just looking presentable, she told herself. There was nothing more to it than that.

After all, the last thing she needed was another heartbreaker. Another man to lift her up and let her down. Another man to pull her attention from the business. From her family's legacy.

Three more children had already arrived by the time Mary made it back to the storefront. She collected their coats while Ben chatted with their parents and showed the girls to the table. She hurried to the back room to hang up the sweet little jackets in bright colors, only to return to the front to find more kids waiting, their faces shining, their parents murmuring. One woman even asked for her card, and it took everything in Mary not to reach out and hug her, but instead to ever so casually pull one from the stack she kept near the cash register.

Soon all the guests had arrived and the parents had cleared out. Mary eyed Ben, waiting for his lead, but he just stared at her blankly. "Is your, um . . . Should we wait for Violet's mother?" she asked. It still wasn't clear what the situation was, not that it should matter to her. It wasn't like she was *interested* in him. Surely she knew better than that!

His expression darkened. His gaze darted sharply to the table where the little girls sat giggling and talking loudly, and then back to hers. "She's not coming," he said in a voice barely above a whisper.

"Oh." Mary nodded quickly. "Okay, then. Let's get the party started!" she smiled brightly and walked over to the table to tell the girls about the party games she'd planned for the day.

Once the girls were all patiently waiting in line for their chance to pin their cherry on the cardboard ice cream sundae she'd taped against the far wall, Mary went to the table to fill each plastic cup with grape juice.

A voice, low and husky in her ear, made her jump, and she sloshed some of the purple liquid over the tablecloth. Her hand darted for the nearest napkin just as Ben's did, and she felt her cheeks burn with a mixture of embarrassment and something far more intense. Something that felt an awful lot like attraction.

"You scared me," she laughed under her breath, feeling flustered. What was it about this man that made her so jumpy? She looked away, eager to get ahold of herself, and gathered the sopping napkins into her hand.

"Sorry about that," he said with a smile when she returned a few seconds later with a fresh stack of napkins. "I just wanted to say thanks. For the games. For all of this. I didn't really think this far ahead."

Mary felt her heart swell, but a flicker of worry creased her brow as she went around the table with the napkins, sure to give one to each girl. There was something about the way he talked, about how nervous he seemed around Violet, a little out of practice and eager to please, that made her curious about the situation.

She set the last napkin down at the head of the table. Not her business. Ben was hardly a friend, and he'd made it clear he wasn't looking to even be neighbors.

She looked up, catching his eyes on hers, and felt her pulse quicken. A shame really. It would have been nice to have a friend across the hall. A friend, and nothing more, she reminded herself, tearing her gaze from those full lips, that straight, strong nose.

"My turn!" Violet cried, interrupting Mary's thoughts.

Happy to have an excuse to leave Ben's unwavering stare for a moment, she hurried over to the group of excited children and helped Violet with the eye mask. Taking her by the shoulders, she spun her around three times and gave her a little push in the right direction, hoping the birthday girl would have luck and take home the prize. Even though she'd been sure to make enough goody bags for each child, she knew that small victories went a long way, and with the way Ben was acting, she couldn't help but sense that something was off. It was the little girl's birthday. Shouldn't her mother be here?

Violet marched to the paper that was taped to the wall, feeling this way and that as Ben edged toward the place where Mary stood watching. "A little to the left," she whispered so softly that she knew Violet couldn't hear. "A little more," she pleaded, wincing as the girl placed the cherry a solid foot from where it belonged.

Violet pulled off her mask and stared at her effort, her small face crumbling when she saw that she hadn't won.

"Oh no," Ben muttered, rolling back on his heels.

Mary flashed him a look of panic and quickly stepped forward. No one cried over a bowl of ice cream. Not in Sunshine Creamery, at least. At home, well, sometimes that was what ice cream was for, she supposed.

"Violet, I was wondering if you might want to come with me to the jukebox to pick a song for the next game," she said.

Violet blinked up at her with interest, and the tears seemed to dry up as quickly as her mouth lifted into a smile. "Okay!" she said, jumping up and down.

Mary reached down to take her hand and glanced back at Ben over her shoulder. The smile he gave her was one of relief, and, if she didn't dare say so, something more.

\*

Ben watched as Mary scooped ice cream into twelve small glass bowls. He couldn't help himself. Every time she bent over, he let his gaze drop to her curves. The tight, small waist, the curve of her hips, the endlessly long legs covered in thick black tights he could almost imagine peeling off, inch by inch . . .

He stiffened. It had been too long. Two years, actually.

He hadn't been with a woman since the divorce. His sister thought he was crazy, that it was part of his problem, urged him to go out, get it out of his system. Lots of men would, he knew. But he was never that way. Dana had been his first love. His college sweetheart. But it hadn't been enough. Not to last a lifetime.

The party was nearly over. Already some parents had arrived to collect their children—faces Ben barely recognized from various events at Violet's school. He'd always thought he'd be one of those dads who volunteered, got involved in helping with sets for the school play, or helped out with the assembly of the new playground equipments on a sunny Saturday afternoon. Instead, he kept to himself. Sat next to his ex at holiday music assemblies, focused on his daughter, learned to look away from the other, happier families, trying not to think of the life he'd wanted for his daughter and hadn't been able to give her.

Mary walked over to him, her smile a little tired. "I think that was a success," she said.

"Let me stay and help you clean up," he said. Sprinkles and chocolate chips were all over the floor, and whipped cream was spilled over the purple tablecloth.

"This won't take me more than ten minutes," she said, brushing away his concern. "Besides, it's all part of the service."

The service. Of course. For a moment it was easy to get caught up in the sweet way she hovered around the girls, encouraged them to dance, made sure there were no tears even when ice cream toppled over or they almost ran out of pink jellybeans.

She was doing her job. And that shouldn't disappoint him. Not in the slightest.

A jolt of panic shot through him when he realized he'd forgotten his checkbook back at the apartment. "Do you take credit cards?" he asked.

"I'm afraid we're cash only." She shrugged. "Just slip it under my door. No problem."

"No," Ben frowned and rubbed his forehead. "I'll write the check tonight. I'm sorry. I wasn't thinking. Violet's mother usually insists on taking care of these things." He supposed it made her feel like she was doing her part, and in that way, she was.

Mary set a hand on his arm. It was light, feminine, but reassuring all at once. He stiffened, unused to this kind of connection, and had the strange desire for it to linger just a little bit longer.

"It's fine, Ben," she said, laughing quietly. He liked the way she said his name. The way she seemed to imply that she knew him. It had been a long time since he'd felt like anyone knew him.

He couldn't even say he knew himself much anymore.

Violet came running up to them, her eyes glazed and shiny from too much sugar consumption, a ring of sticky chocolate sauce covering her mouth and cheeks. "I had fun," she announced.

"I can see you did," Ben remarked, grinning. Mission

accomplished. Now to make sure that tomorrow, on her actual birthday, he could say the same. "Be sure to thank Mary for giving you such a nice party."

"Thank you, Mary," Violet said dutifully, and then, to his surprise and horror, flung herself at Mary's waist.

Mary let out a little whoop of surprise and hugged Violet in return, but Ben could only cringe as he saw the dark stain appear on the waist of her soft, pastel sweater. He walked back behind the counter, grabbed some paper towels and wetted them.

Violet was already profusely apologizing by the time he made it back around. "Here," he said, pressing it to the smudge just above her hip. Mary lifted her hands in surprise as Ben worked at removing the stain, his head bent in concentration, ignoring Mary's protests and Violet's insistence that it was just an accident.

His hand suddenly stilled and he looked up to catch Mary's eye, hoping he hadn't upset her, only to find that her gaze danced with amusement, and something else, something deeper. Something a lot like . . . interest.

Tensing, he thrust the paper towel into her hand. "Sorry. I just didn't want it to set."

"It's fine," Mary said, her voice catching. She cleared her throat and broke his stare. "Good as new," she informed Violet, whose mouth had turned downward at her mistake.

"You're not mad?"

"It's just chocolate," Mary said gaily. "I work in an ice

cream shop. This happens all the time."

"You're not going to go away then?" Violet whispered.

Mary frowned and slanted a glance at Ben. Ben ran a hand through his hair, gritting his teeth until his jaw hurt. "Where would I go? I live right across the hall from your dad."

Violet looked up at Ben, unconvinced.

"Can I offer you a ride home?" Ben asked Mary.

"Oh, no, it's fine. I can walk." Mary began straightening chairs.

"But it's twenty-eight degrees outside," Ben said, even though he knew this was an excuse, and an exceptionally convenient one. For the second time since Violet had come to stay with him, their day was a little happier, a little brighter. He wasn't ready for that to end just yet. "I'm driving you."

Mary stopped straightening up and gave him a long look. "Okay, then. Thank you."

But something in him told him that the gratitude was all his.

*

Mary held the door open while Ben carried Violet into the mailroom of the apartment building. One of her sparkly pink shoes was slipping off her foot, and Mary reached out to catch it just before it fell from her toe.

"Sugar overdose?" she asked Ben.

He gave a wry smile. "More like lack of sleep. I let her stay up last night and watch a movie, and I'm guessing too much excitement for today kept her awake long after I'd tucked her in."

Mary reached for the door to the stairwell, feeling herself cringe when she noticed her handy little sign for the community yard sale, still taped to the glass. Not a single name was on the list other than her own. On to plan B, she supposed. Whatever that was.

"I've been meaning to take that down," she said, reddening.

"You shouldn't," Ben said, catching her by surprise. He hesitated, shifted Violet on his hip, and squared her with a look. His lashes were dark and curly. How had she not noticed that before? She supposed she'd been too focused on the murky blue eyes underneath, trying to read them, to understand him a little better. "It's a good idea. I would participate myself if I had anything left to give away. My ex ended up with most of my worldly possessions." He grinned, but there was a flicker of something sad in his eyes.

So there it was. His ex.

"Well, I think you raised a good point about the weather." Mary shrugged and carefully removed the sign from the door, sure not to leave any strips of tape. "I keep hoping the sun will come out one day and melt all this snow. It's bad for business." Now it was her turn to give a wry smile.

"I hope today helped," Ben said. "No doubt the kids will want their parents to take them back."

Mary nodded enthusiastically. "Every little bit helps, and I appreciate it. A lot. I just need to figure out how to keep things going during the winter months going forward." She put on a brave smile, as if she had everything under control, when in fact she did not. Not in the least. She opened the door a little wider, "After you."

"Normally I'd say ladies first, but thanks. Violet's getting a little heavy," Ben said, laughing.

"Is she . . . your only child?" Mary asked.

"We'd thought about having more, but that never happened." Ben's brow furrowed as he brushed by her and began ascending the staircase, Violet never moving the entire time.

Mary followed him closely to the landing and reached into her handbag for her key. "Thanks for the ride home. You saved me a walk in the cold."

"Do you mind doing me a favor?" Ben asked, his eyebrow lifting in invitation.

Mary's curiosity piqued. "Sure."

"My keys are in my pocket and . . ." He dipped his head, motioning to Violet, whom he was clinging to with both arms.

Mary laughed. "Of course!" She eyed his jeans, dark and a little tight, that clung to his perfectly sculpted thighs and felt her stomach do a little dance. It had been so long since she'd touched a man, especially one that was as good looking as Ben. She'd do it quickly, in and out, no different than she might touch, say, her sister. She let out a shaky breath and inched her fingers toward his front pocket, stopping when Ben cleared his throat.

"The um, *coat* pocket," he said, his lips curving with mischief.

"Oh." Mary blinked. "Of course. Of course." *Silly girl.* Of course they'd be in his coat pocket. She pushed back the swell of disappointment as she sunk her hand into the wool, her hands going nowhere near those sexy parts, reminding herself that this was for the best. There was no point in fancying the man, after all. He was her neighbor. And the last thing she needed was more complication in her life.

What she needed was a nice, friendly man next door. A man who watered her plants on occasion—should she decide to take on such a responsibility at some point. A man who said hello when he passed her in the hallway.

What she didn't need was temptation. And really, that's all he was.

She turned the key in the lock and the door swung open. In all the months she'd lived here, she'd never caught a glimpse inside, not a hint of insight into his world, but now, in a matter of days, she was finding that there was a lot more to the man than first met the eye.

She hovered in the hallway as Ben stepped over dolls and picture books and deposited Violet over the back of the brown leather couch in a touchingly tender way.

"She'll probably sleep for the rest of the afternoon," Ben said, walking back to the door.

Mary pulled her eyes from the apartment, from the

bare furnishings and mess of pink and sparkly girly toys, and looked up into Ben's gaze. His hair was disheveled, his eyes a little wild, but his smile had never seemed easier.

"You don't want to forget this," Mary said, handing over Violet's shoe.

"Thanks," Ben said. "For . . . everything."

"It was my pleasure," Mary said, backing up to slip her key into her own door. She held up a hand, her heart tugging as Ben did the same, and then disappeared into her apartment.

The man had forgotten to pay her. And somehow, she didn't even care.

# Chapter Seven

Ben checked his phone for the eleventh time that hour and, heaving a sigh, shoved it back into his pocket. The wind was strong when he pushed open the door, but the chill had subsided a bit.

Coming around the car, he opened the back passenger door and grinned at Violet. "Ready for dinner, birthday girl?"

"Why hasn't Mommy called yet?" she asked in response.

Ben gritted his teeth. Hell if he knew. It was already half past four, and ten thirty in London. Dana had let the entire day go by without a phone call, but there was no overlooking the huge package that had arrived yesterday, with every toy Violet could ever ask for.

Where was she? And what could be more important

than her daughter?

He ground his teeth a little deeper. He knew the answer to that.

"Let's go inside and have fun. I think Grandma made you a cake!" He helped Violet out of her car seat, refusing to let his expression match Violet's concern. This was her birthday, and he might not have given her the biggest present, but he was here, and so help him, this day would be special.

Just being here, on the North Shore, in his childhood neighborhood made him feel a little better. He knew he should come back more often, spend time in the house that was the only thing left he had of a home, surrounded by people who cared, who would always be there. It was just difficult sometimes—to work up the energy for the drive, to go back to where he'd come from, to face another setup, he thought wryly.

No doubt he would be spared a blind date tonight. It was Violet's birthday, after all, and besides, his mother respected the fact that she'd had enough change in her life recently. She didn't need random new people floating in and out of it, too.

The door to the brick Colonial home swung open before Ben and Violet had even made it to the front stoop. His parents stood side by side, holding a big bunch of balloons, their smiles ones of pure joy as they swooped down to give their only grandchild a hug. Ben spotted Emma over his mother's shoulder, her expression a little more subdued.

"How's the hermit?" she asked, giving him a knowing smile.

"Shouldn't I be asking you that?" he shot back. "You haven't called me in all of two days. I was beginning to worry something had happened to you."

Emma did a poor job of hiding her smile. "Point made." She stood back, giving him an overt once-over. "You look better than usual. Less grim."

"It's Violet's birthday," he reminded her, as they all moved into the front hall.

Emma tipped her head, wrinkling her nose the way she had since they were kids. "No, it's not that. It's something else. Or maybe . . . *Someone* else." She waggled her eyebrows.

Ben took off his coat and draped it on the bench next to the old grandfather's clock that chimed on the hour. "That someone is standing right there. She's about four feet tall."

Emma shrugged, showing she wasn't convinced, and then left him to greet her niece. Younger than himself by three years and without a relationship or child of her own, he continued to find it pretty damn rich that she was so keen on giving him unsolicited advice, but then, that was just Emma. She'd always been opinionated. Always been mature beyond her years.

His mother helped Violet out of her coat, and soon, they were all gathered in the big formal dining room at the front of the house, which was filled with streamers and even more balloons.

"Look at that cake!" Ben shook his head at the unicorn shaped dessert. "You really outdid yourself, Mom."

His mother brushed a hand through the air, but he could see that she was pleased at the compliment. "I was happy to do it." Lowering her voice, she said, "This can't be easy for her. I wanted this day to be special."

"It is," he said firmly. It would be. He pulled his phone from his pocket and checked the screen. Still no call.

"Well," his mother said, as she pulled out the chair at the head of the table, typically reserved for Ben's dad, but today clearly reserved for Violet. "Who's in the mood for pizza?"

Ben met is sister's eyes and laughed. The one day he thought he could get away from his usual routine, and he was right back in it. Only tonight he wouldn't let things slide too far into the familiar. Tonight was Violet's night. He didn't need to hear any concern, not unless it was for his daughter.

His gut knotted when he checked his watch. She had to call. If she didn't . . . He pulled in a breath. She would call. She had to.

His dad set the pizza boxes on the center of the table and set a slice on Violet's plate. Ben took his old seat, the one across from his sister, wondering if he would ever get used to the empty chair beside him where Dana used to sit. It wasn't that he missed her presence, not anymore. It was that he hated the reminder of it, of a time and period that had come and gone, of the void in his life where none was supposed to be.

His mother took the chair next to Emma, where Violet usually sat, and began asking conversationally about the birthday party.

"We made our own sundaes," Violet told her. "And Mary let us each pick a song from the jukebox."

"Mary?" Emma cocked an eyebrow and nailed him with a look.

"She's the ice cream lady. She's really pretty. She lives next door to Daddy," Violet added.

Ben mentally rolled his eyes as his sister's gaze grew wider. *Thank you, Violet.* As usual, her lack of discretion shone through.

"I see," Emma said, her eyes sparkling. "And does this Mary woman have a husband?"

Ben set down his fork. "For God's sake—"

"No!" Violet cried happily. "She doesn't even have a boyfriend. My friends and I asked."

Emma nodded thoughtfully as she reached for a slice of pizza. "No boyfriend. And pretty, too." She lifted her gaze to Ben. "What do you think about that?"

"I don't think there's anything to think about," Ben replied, and crammed the pizza into his mouth.

Except he did think about it. Thought about those big round eyes when they met his gaze, thought about the sweet pink mouth that curved into that beautiful smile. He thought about the sound of her laugh. And the way he felt when he heard it.

He thought about Mary quite a bit, actually.

And that was just the problem.

*

Mary sat in her sister's dining room, leafing through another bridal magazine.

"You're not going to make me wear chartreuse, are you?" she teased, as Lila set three plates at the table.

"I was thinking mustard yellow would be better with your coloring." Lila winked, and disappeared into the kitchen again.

Mary sighed. There had been a time so recently when she'd dared to imagine planning her own wedding . . . to Jason, of all people. She pursed her lips as she flicked to the next page. No use wallowing in that disappointment. Not when she had so many more on the horizon.

The threat of losing Sunshine Creamery seemed all too possible now. She didn't have much left to pour into the business, not to mention any repairs the building itself called for. She was barely covering her own rent. Summer might pick up, but what about next winter? Her stomach ached just thinking about it.

"Any more thoughts on your dress?" Mary asked when Lila returned with a bottle of white wine. She needed to stay focused in the moment, not catastrophize the situation. She deserved a night of fun. God knew the rest of her nights were spent worrying, scheming. But she was running out of ideas, and the ones she'd come up with, like the yard sale, felt a little desperate.

Lila glanced over her shoulder at Sam, who was still in the kitchen. "No, but I'm glad you brought it up. Do you remember how much we loved looking at Mom and Dad's wedding photo growing up?"

Mary hadn't thought of that photo in years. It was faded, the colors muted, protected by the silver frame Gram kept on the mantle. "We loved how young they looked."

"Mom was so pretty," Lila said sadly, and Mary set her hand on her sister's arm. They didn't talk of their parents often. They'd been raised by their grandparents since they were children, and somehow the recent passing of their grandfather had hit them the hardest, awakening the realization that all they had left was each other.

Except now Lila would have Sam, too. Mary swallowed hard, not wanting to go down that path. Maybe someday she'd find the right man, too. But for now, she had to stay focused on their family's legacy. Just thinking of her grandfather reinforced her determination.

"I wanted to see how you felt about it, but . . . I was thinking I might wear Mom's dress. If it fits."

Mary blinked. As children they had begged to try it on, and their grandmother would let them, only for a few minutes. They'd stand in the gown, twisting and turning in front of the floor-length mirror that hung on the back of their bedroom door, feeling so special. Eventually the novelty had worn off, and they'd stopped trying it on, and eventually, Mary realized with a bit of a start, stopped thinking of it all.

"I think that is a wonderful idea," Mary said, her voice a little thick.

"I won't keep it," Lila said quickly. "It can be ours, to share. If you want it someday."

Mary pulled back in her chair, covering her emotions with a giant roll of her eyes. "Given my luck with men, I can't really think that far ahead."

"Well, you never know. Look at me and Sam." Lila gave a sly grin and Mary just shook her head as Sam came into the room to join them. Mary looked at the table, at the beautiful dinner her sister and her fiancé had made, and knew that it was probably in her honor. She felt touched, and guilty as hell.

Her sister had always looked out for her growing up, showing strength and courage after their parents had died, and all these years later she was still doing it, taking on a role she didn't need to fill but wanted to. Mary wished for once she could do the same.

And she could. By keeping Sunshine Creamery afloat. And by not worrying Lila with the tricky details like lack of customers and the threat of the building falling apart on her, piece by piece.

They ate their dinner, chatting about wedding plans and Lila and Sam's advertising agency. Mary tried to keep the conversation on them, but they were too polite. Too vested.

*Too caring*, she thought sadly.

"How's the shop?"

Even though Mary knew her sister was just showing interest in her life, she felt her defenses prickle. "Good," she said, taking a sip from her wine, hoping the chill would drive the heat from her face. "I hosted a birthday party yesterday," she offered, happy to have something worthwhile to report. "One of my neighbors has a six-year-old," she said. "Everything was purple."

Lila stabbed a piece of broccoli with her fork. "Which neighbor?"

"Oh . . ." She tried to keep her tone casual, but she struggled to make eye contact. "The one across the hall," Mary said, setting down her wine glass.

Lila frowned. "The unfriendly one?"

Mary bristled and reached for her fork. "Oh, now . . . I wouldn't say he's all that unfriendly."

Lila scoffed and stared at Mary until she had her full, if not reluctant, attention. "Mary, he yanked down one of the signs you put in the lobby."

Mary considered this. Indeed, he had done that, and she had been quite peeved at the time. "Well, in fairness, he might have been following my suggestion a little too closely," she said, recalling the cheery letter she'd hung up about keeping the junk mail in the recycling bin and not littered around the floor near the old radiator.

"He has barely grunted a hello at you in months. Unless he treats you differently when I'm not around." Lila raised an eyebrow, and Mary shifted her eyes, feeling suddenly like she was on trial. "It's too bad. He's sort of cute, if you like the silent and broody type," Lila said, resuming her dinner. "But he's not very nice."

Mary chewed on her lip. So she hadn't just imagined it. He was cute. Damn cute.

Not that it mattered.

"I don't think it's that he isn't nice," she said pensively. "I think it's that he's . . . troubled."

Sam let out a whoop of laughter, and Lila nailed her with a long, hard look. "Troubled?" She pinched her lips. "Cute and troubled. Please don't go near that, Mary. Promise me."

"Of course not!" Mary insisted, but her voice felt shrill, even to her own ears, and she had a sudden feeling that she was lying. Not just to her sister. But to herself.

She had enough trouble. More than her sister or Sam knew or would ever know. And the last thing she needed was any more of it.

She'd try to remember that the next time Ben flashed her one of his elusive—and heart fluttering—smiles.

*

The phone call came just as Ben was pulling to a stop in front of the apartment building. He knew it was her before he even glanced at the screen. Anger coursed through his blood when he saw the name, and he connected the call with the punch of his thumb.

"It's about time," was all he said. He glanced in the rearview mirror. Violet was sound asleep, her snores soft over her steady breath. "You missed her birthday, Dana," he hissed. "You missed her birthday."

"If you knew the day I had—"

"I don't really care about the day you had," he said, his voice catching with fresh anger. "I care about the little girl who waited all day for the phone to ring. She's asleep."

"Can you wake her?"

He wanted to say no, teach his ex a lesson once and for all, but he didn't want to break his daughter's heart any more than it had already been broken. "I'll have her call you back in five minutes," he said, and disconnected the call.

Cursing under his breath, he climbed out of the car and came around to Violet's side. She protested when he tried to rouse her, but as soon as he told her that her mother had called, her eyes sprung open wide.

"We'll call her back once we're inside," he promised.

He sighed heavily as Violet ran all the way to the building and up the three flights of stairs to the door. Once she was settled on the couch, he dialed the number and handed her the phone. He closed his eyes at her squeal of joy when the call went through.

He didn't know why it continued to disappoint him. Why it was okay for Dana to come and go, to break promises, to break hearts. That she was rewarded by the simple efforts, by material objects, as if love could be bought, not just earned.

He shook away the thought. Dana was her mother. Violet should adore her. But it didn't stop him from wanting more for his daughter.

While Violet chatted away about school and her friends, Ben wrote out a check for Mary, chastising himself for taking this long to get it to her. He was overwhelmed, stressed, and not entirely himself these days. But that was no excuse. The truth was he had thought about Mary. More than he should. And he'd been resisting another encounter with her, resisting the way he felt when he was around her.

He opened his door and stood in the small hallway, listening for any signs of life behind the solid wood door that divided his world from hers.

With any luck he could just slip it under her door. Transaction made. Business finished.

Just in case, he tapped on the door. Softly.

He held his breath. No sound. Ignoring the twinge of disappointment, he crouched to slide the check when the door swung open. Ben glanced up, his eyes latching onto bare legs that he traced as he brought himself to a standing position. Mary's eyes were bright and inquisitive, her full lips pulled into a small smile. "Hello," she said, with a cute little tip of her head.

She was wearing a long T-shirt, some kind of pajamas, he supposed. He forced his eyes to stay on hers, not to stray back to those long, smooth legs.

"I have your check," he said, thrusting it at her. "Sorry for the delay."

"No problem," she said. She folded it in half, not even looking at the sum.

Ben frowned slightly. She trusted him. To bring the money. To do the right thing. Or maybe she just knew where to find him.

He rolled back on his heels. Something told him Mary would have been happy to do the party for free, out of the goodness of her heart, and that . . . well, he wasn't really sure what to do with that.

"How was work today?" he asked conversationally, not yet ready to turn and leave, go back to his apartment, not when she was standing here looking so pretty, so accessible, so . . . friendly.

He supposed it was ironic that the one quality that had so annoyed him was the one he'd come to value the most about her. Come to depend on, really.

He swallowed hard. You couldn't depend on anyone. Only yourself. It was a lesson he'd learned the hard way. One Violet had, too.

"Slow. A little stressful." Mary heaved a sigh. "No new developments. I'm hoping things hold out until the end of the summer, when I've socked more away for repairs."

"I might be able to help," he offered, feeling his pulse skip on the statement.

Her eyes flashed on his. "Oh, no, I can't take your money."

He laughed. It felt good. "No, I meant, I could stop by one day this week and take a look at the damage. I'm a contractor," he explained, leaving it at that. He'd been trained as one, but he'd transitioned to project management years ago. Still, he was more than capable of assessing a situation and knowing what it would cost.

The first genuine smile of the night broke her face, and Ben swallowed hard at the sight. Her pink lips curved at the corners, and her eyes danced. "This feels like fate! I mean, not in the *fate* fate sort of way." She reddened. "I just mean . . . thank you."

"My pleasure," Ben said easily. Really, it was no trouble, and given his position to help, he was hardly in a position not to offer it. Not with the kindness she'd shown Violet.

She was a nice girl, if not an extremely attractive one, too, and his sister was right. He did need to join the land of the living again. Most of his buddies from the single days were married with kids now, most had flown to the burbs, and grabbing a drink with those that remained only revealed that heaviness in his chest. He wasn't interested in the bar scene. Didn't want to be dragged along to check out women, or even to chat them up. But a little friendly exchange with a neighbor was surprisingly pleasing. And it was innocent enough. It would have to be.

# Chapter Eight

Mary couldn't remember the last time she'd dressed up to go to work at Sunshine Creamery. Usually she was happy with a pastel-colored sundress in the summer, or a practical sweater and skirt or jeans in the fall and winter.

But today, Ben was stopping by, and that made things, well . . . special.

She'd slept in, something she rarely did, and took far too much time brushing her hair and experimenting with various shades of lip gloss. Having skipped breakfast, she treated herself to a latte and muffin from the Corner Beanery. Hardly a healthy lunch, but it kept her on budget, and what her sister didn't know wouldn't hurt her. If Lila didn't think Mary was eating three healthy meals a day, she got twitchy.

Mary grinned as she bent to rest her paper cup and bag

on the stoop of Sunshine Creamery so she could pull the key free from her pocket and unlock the door. It was fun to mess with Lila a bit, every now and then, when it didn't constitute as genuinely worrying her about anything serious. She still got a laugh when she thought of the horror in her sister's face when Mary told her she'd eaten nothing but ice cream straight from the carton one night for dinner. Honestly, why dirty a bowl? And really, why bother to cook? And after all, wasn't ice cream her specialty?

Someday, she supposed, she would have someone to eat dinner with, like her sister did.

Someone like Ben.

She brushed that thought away quickly, scooped up her coffee and pastry bag, and flipped the sign on the door. It was already half past eleven and even though she doubted she'd see a customer all day, she felt the need to prepare today's flavor. Somehow, not following through with her normal routine felt like giving up.

And she couldn't quit on Gramps. After all, he'd never quit on them.

The snow was beginning to melt, but Mary was almost too scared to check the forecast. A little bit of ignorance went a long way in helping her mood at times. And what was the point in worrying about tomorrow when you still had to get through today? She had enough to worry about for the next few hours. Things like pipes and codes and surprise inspections . . . and Ben's deep blue eyes and those oh so kissable lips.

Well. That was about enough crazy talk for one morning!

Mary set to work on a batch of strawberry shortcake ice cream, even though it was more of a summer flavor, and wrote it out on the big chalkboard sign she then dragged out to the sidewalk. She craned her eyes to the sun, listening to water pellets slide from rooftops onto the street below, and felt a flutter in her chest. *It can only get better from here*, she told herself. Spring would come, and soon. But would it be enough?

She checked her watch again. Ben would be here any minute now. She turned back to the shop, for once grateful for the lack of traffic, and then wondered how she might busy herself when he came in. The place was spotless. There was no ice cream to make. She could pay bills, but oh . . . She set a hand to her stomach. She'd deal with that tomorrow.

"Hello there."

Mary jumped at the deep, smooth voice, a smile curving her mouth before she even turned to look at the owner.

"You're early," she said, allowing herself a brief glance up and down his perfect form.

Yep. Hot. She was sort of hoping he'd show up looking much worse than he did in her mind. When she thought of him, that was . . .

"Is that okay? I wanted to get an early start before I pick up Violet," he explained, lifting his toolbox.

"Are you kidding me? It's more than okay. I really can't thank you enough for stopping by to take a look at things. I'm sort of bracing myself for bad news, though."

"Let me see what's going on." His mouth quirked into a lopsided grin and he gave her a reassuring pat on the shoulder. *Well, that was certainly friendly of him*, Mary thought. If she didn't know better, she would say the man was definitely warming up to her.

Mary couldn't hide her smile as she followed him back into the painfully empty ice cream parlor and led him to the back room. "This is where they replaced the pipe," she said, pointing up to the gaping hole in the ceiling. She walked to her desk and ruffled through the papers until she found what she was looking for. "And this is the estimate I received. Well, one of them. They all say the same, more or less."

They all said she was in big trouble.

Ben glanced at the estimate, giving a low whistle. "No more leaks?" he asked.

Mary shook her head. "No, but I'm worried about inspections. Or another one busting. They said the pipes aren't up to code. My grandfather bought this place so long ago, and at some point, he must have stopped thinking about maintenance."

Ben opened his toolbox and took out a flashlight. "Do you have a ladder?"

"I have a chair," Mary offered, and dragged the wooden one over from her desk.

Ben climbed up and shone his light, craning his neck

as he studied the pipes through the hole. Mary held her breath, waiting for the bad news to fall, but she was momentarily distracted by the hint of skin that flickered as Ben lifted his arm, pulling his shirt up in the process. His stomach was smooth and hard, and she felt something deep within her rouse.

She looked away quickly. Enough of that. It was one thing to look. It was another to stare.

And another to lust. Yes, lusting was completely unacceptable.

Finally, he sighed and jumped off. "Well, these are old, and the truth is you do face the risk of more problems if you don't do something about it. "He tucked the flashlight back into the box and looked at her squarely. "Do you want the good news or the bad?"

Mary held her breath, daring to hope that meant the news wasn't too bad. Either that or he enjoyed playing with her emotions. Both were entirely possible.

"The bad news first." She wouldn't be able to enjoy the good news knowing something worse was following it.

"Your pipes are not up to code, and the plumber was probably right about the one not holding up if we get another sub-zero day."

Mary felt her heart sink. "The good news now, please?" she asked weakly.

"The good news is that unless you plan to do a major construction project anytime soon, I don't think you need to worry about redoing all the plumbing. And another piece of good news is that the leaves are starting to bud on the trees. It's mid-March. I don't think you need to worry about another frozen pipe for a while."

"Oh, thank God," Mary gushed, and fought the urge to fling her arms around his neck. It's what she would have done with a friend, or even Sam, but Ben wasn't quite a friend yet. She wasn't sure what he was, actually. But somehow, he was beginning to feel like more than just a neighbor.

"I have a feeling the people who came in to give you quotes were using scare tactics." He arched a brow as he picked up his toolbox. "They knew an opportunity when they saw one."

Mary pursed her lips. She didn't like the thought of men assuming she didn't know a thing about plumbing just because she had girl parts, even if, admittedly, she didn't know a thing about plumbing. Never really cared to, honestly. It was much more fun to make ice cream, and serve it to smiling customers. Now that she was a business owner, though, she'd need to learn these things.

"Replacing a pipe is more doable than ripping out everything. I'll call the contractor back tomorrow, just in case we get another cold front."

He looked at her quizzically. "I'll have one of my guys stop by and do it tonight. We'll get this ceiling patched up, too."

"What? I mean, no, the money . . . I don't have it yet."

"Consider it a gift," he said casually.

"No. I mean, no, no, you've done enough. I can't."
Mary blinked, feeling herself stiffen. A smile here and
there was one thing, but this? This was a leap, something
far bigger than she could have expected from the man
who up until a couple weeks ago wouldn't even make eye
contact with her.

"It's really not a big deal." Ben slid her a slow smile
that made her heart beat a little faster. "I'll oversee it
myself, even. What time do you close?"

"Seven. Nine in the summer."

"We'll take care of it after you've closed then, so we
don't disrupt the customers."

Mary itched to point out that there probably wouldn't
be any customers to disrupt, but instead said, "Thank
you. You don't know how much I appreciate this. I might
be able to sleep through the night tonight thanks to you."

His mouth quirked, and Mary felt her heart begin to
pound, suddenly imagining him asleep just across the hall,
a mere set of doors separating his body from hers.

She startled suddenly. "Wait. Violet. Won't she need to
go to bed?"

Ben closed his eyes and rubbed a hand over his face. "I
wasn't even thinking." He pulled in a breath and blew it
out slowly. "Up until recently she lived with her mother. I
guess you could say I got used to be being a bachelor
again," he admitted sheepishly.

Mary hesitated, and then decided to go for it. "I
wouldn't mind watching her tonight."

Ben frowned. "Oh, no, I wouldn't want to impose."

"Impose? You're the one doing me the favor, remember?"

He considered this. "If you're sure . . . She likes you. I think she'd really like that."

"She's a sweet girl, Ben. I'm looking forward to it, really." Mary set a hand on his arm; it felt warm and thick under her fingers. She wondered if he would pull it back, stiffen, but something about it felt right, like they'd just made another baby step toward . . . something.

*

Ben could hear the sound of giggling through the door before he'd even set his foot on the carpeted landing that separated his apartment from Mary's. He paused, wrapping his hand around the key in his pocket, enjoying the sweet sound, almost not daring to move. Things with Violet were still fragile. More than he wanted them to be. More than he could bear.

But something had shifted, giving him a hope that the dark times might be sliding behind him at long last, that tomorrow might be a little brighter than today.

Grinning at another peal of muffled laughter he recognized as Violet's, Ben turned the lock and opened the door a crack, poking his head around to see his daughter dancing around the room in one of her sparkly tutus, waving a wand at Mary, who also seemed to be covered in some sort of glittering pink material. "Hello!" he called out, wondering where he fit into all the fun, and hating the thought of interrupting it.

Mary turned, and blushed when she caught his eye. Slowly, she unraveled her legs and stood, revealing a hilariously small tutu that jutted out from her hips. Ben dropped his gaze a little farther, taking in the long sweep of her thighs that were covered in tight black leggings, and swallowed hard.

"Cute skirt." Ben grinned.

"Violet insisted," Mary said, her cheeks flushing deeper with her defense as she swept her hands over the sparkling netted material.

Ben met her gaze. "I'm not complaining."

Mary's cheeks grew a notch pinker. She adjusted the tiara on her head and motioned to the coffee table, which was covered in pink and purple plastic dishes. "We were just finishing up our tea party, unless you'd care to join us?"

"I'd love to, but I think it's someone's bedtime," Ben said, giving Violet a knowing look.

Violet groaned. "But we were playing princess!"

Ben started to open up his mouth, but Mary held up hand, silencing him. She bent down until she was eye to eye with Violet, taking the little girl's hands. "But you know what they say about princesses, don't you?" She made a big show of leaning in to stage whisper in Violet's ear: "They need their beauty sleep."

Violet giggled, but she still didn't look convinced. "I was having fun," she said, starting to pout.

"So was I, and that just means we'll have to do it again sometime. I'm right across the hall." Mary pointed to the front door of the apartment, and Violet followed her movement, mollified.

Ben felt the first prickle of panic, tensing at the transition that was happening, the attachment that Violet was forming to Mary, but then he saw how quickly her mood was turned around, the smile that lit up her face, and he felt something in him soften.

"Can Mary tuck me in?" Violet asked.

Ben eyed the firm clasp his daughter had of Mary's hand and met her eyes, hoping she sensed the apology in his expression. "If she doesn't mind."

"I can think of nothing better!" Mary beamed, and let Violet pull her into the hallway by the hand. She looked back over her shoulder just before they disappeared into Violet's purple and pink bedroom, to flash Ben a smile.

His pulse hitched and something in his gut stirred. It was just a smile, he told himself firmly. But, oh, it was a pretty one. One he wouldn't mind seeing again. And soon.

He tidied up Violet's toys while Mary went through the bedtime routine of helping Violet to brush her teeth and pick out a stuffed animal to sleep with. He waved a critical eye over the room as Mary came back through the hall. Despite his efforts, it still looked like a bachelor pad. He knew it. He was sure Mary knew. And he had the sinking sensation that Violet knew it too.

Mary's eyes were bright, but she looked a bit tired as

she came down the hall.

"I'm happy to report that you are not in any danger of that pipe bursting," he said.

Mary visibly relaxed. "I can't thank you enough."

Ben held up a hand. "No thanks needed. You gave my daughter a wonderful birthday party last weekend. It's the least I can do."

Mary hesitated, and then nodded once. "Well. It's late. I should let you get some rest."

Ben stiffened, not ready for her to leave just yet, even though he knew he should agree, bid her good night, pour a beer, and turn on the television. This was his routine. But she was shaking it up, challenging him.

"You could stay," he blurted. He cleared his throat. "I mean, there's no need to rush off. Maybe . . . Would you like something to drink?"

Wow. It had been even longer than he'd realized since he'd been in the dating scene. Had it always been this hard to extend an invitation to a woman?

He stopped himself right there. This wasn't a date. It was just a drink with a neighbor.

He looked at Mary. She looked just as panicked as he felt and his heart began to drum as he waited for her response, his rational side silently pleading with her to make up a polite excuse, turn him down gently, let him be on his way, but the other part of him was almost hoping she'd say yes, that he wouldn't have to spend another night alone.

He thought of his sister, grinning wryly. If she could see him now.

"Oh. Um." Mary bit her lip, her eyes shifting to the left.

A strange twinge of disappointment settled squarely in his chest, but he backed up, thrusting his hands in his pockets. He hadn't been exactly welcoming until now. Emma's words of warning began to sound loud and clear. There was a consequence to every action—and inaction—in life, and this was one of them.

"I guess that might be nice," she finished, her lips pulling into a shy smile as she met his gaze.

He stared at her for a moment, sensing the shift. Things were changing. Things were different. And he'd almost dare to say, they were better. "Beer or wine?"

"Wine would be perfect."

"I hope Violet wasn't too much trouble," Ben said, as he walked over to the kitchen. "She's been going through some stuff. It hasn't been an easy time for her lately."

"She's really adorable, Ben," Mary said, leaning onto the counter.

Ben uncorked a bottle of red wine and took two glasses down from the cabinet. It occurred to him that it was the first time he'd had proper company in all the time since he'd moved in. He'd gotten used to being on his own.

It may have been comfortable, but it wasn't healthy. And he hadn't been happy, he knew. Just like he knew that he hadn't smiled as much in two years as he had since he'd gotten to know Mary.

"Do you mind me asking . . ." She hesitated, fingered the stem of her wine glass as he filled it.

"Violet's mother?" Ben cocked an eyebrow, and Mary gave a small smile. "It's okay. She's in London, actually."

"Oh, on a business trip?" Mary took a sip of her wine and leaned into the breakfast bar.

Ben considered the question. "You could say that. Except that it doesn't have an end date." He shook his head, feeling the anger course through his blood when he thought of Violet's small voice every time she talked to Dana on the phone, always telling her how much she missed her, always asking when she'd come home. "Dana has always traveled a lot for work. She was gone for six months when Violet was a year old. You'd think we'd be used to it by now," he said bitterly.

"That must be hard on Violet," Mary said, frowning.

The compassion in her eyes made his chest swell. "Very. She keeps asking when she'll come back. You should see the way she lights up when Dana calls. For her sake, I do hope that Dana comes back soon, but only if she'd be willing to commit this time. Though, I have to say that I'm happy to have her here with me." *For many reasons*, he thought to himself. "After the divorce, I only got her a handful of nights a week. It wasn't easy." Now . . . now that would change. Violet needed a secure routine. He was willing to provide that.

"I'm surprised I never noticed Violet in the building

before," Mary said, following him into the living room. She dropped onto the couch easily, and eyed him with growing curiosity as he hovered at the edge and finally took the seat next to her. "But then, I only just moved in and I guess my hours can be a little strange. Even though it's slow this time of year, I feel like I've been at the shop more than ever these past few months." She chewed her lip pensively.

"That shop means a lot to you," he observed.

"It's my family's business. It's all I have left of my grandparents. I'm afraid I'm in a little over my head, though." She gave him a wry smile. "It's why I was crying that night."

"Are things really that bad?" He frowned and thought about how empty the place was every time he'd stopped by. He supposed things could be worse than he'd considered.

"Let's just say that I'm living on hope and denial, and I'm running out of both quickly." Mary shook her head. "Sunshine Creamery was already in a bad place when I took over. Maybe there just isn't a market for it."

Ben thought about Sullivan Construction. If the situation were reversed, he knew he'd be fighting like hell to keep it going.

"Have you ever thought about trying something new, branching out? Selling more than ice cream, maybe mixing things up a bit?"

Mary frowned. "Oh, no. That place has so much history. I freshened up the décor and added new flavors, but I want to keep it authentic."

Ben nodded. "I won't argue. Not if you feel strongly about it."

"Not everyone gets that," Mary said, glancing at him. "I was dating this guy . . . and, let's just say he couldn't understand why I poured so much into the place. Lately, I've been wondering if he was right."

"If something is important to you, then you have to try and fight for it," Ben said. "That's how I felt with my ex. It wasn't working. It hadn't in a long time, but it meant something to me. It was . . . important."

Mary tipped her head. "She lost a good guy."

Ben's breath stilled as he stared into Mary's eyes, his chest growing tight. Her lips were full, rosy and pink, and parted ever so softly into a smile. He swallowed hard, fighting the urge to lean in, to run his hand over her waist, to feel her curves under the soft material of her sweater, to taste those lips, feel her heart.

Her lashes fluttered in surprise as he edged toward her, his heart pounding as the distance between them grew shorter. Jolting, he pulled back, reached up and plucked the tiara off Mary's head, and handed it over to her to her, joking, "I could have let you wear that thing all night, but I don't that that would have been very fair of me."

"I didn't even know Violet had slipped that on my head." Mary patted her hair, laughing nervously. Ben reached for his wine, pulling back against the couch cushion, waiting for his pulse to settle.

Mary took the last sip of her wine and set the glass on the coffee table amongst the plastic tea set that Ben would probably pick up in the morning. "I should really get some beauty sleep myself," she joked, and Ben smiled, half relieved, half disappointed. His heart felt as heavy as his gut, and he knew he should be thankful for the near miss, but a strange part of him wasn't.

He'd almost kissed her, damn it. And if the opportunity arose again, he wasn't so sure he'd be able to resist next time.

# Chapter Nine

Mary's eyes sprung open at the unfamiliar sound coming from somewhere behind her curtains. She blinked, straining to listen again, to see if it had been part of a dream, but no, there it was. The unmistakable, joyous sound of a bird. A bird chirping outside her bedroom window.

Her heart soaring, Mary tossed back the duvet and sprung out of bed, just in time to pull back the curtains and see the little grey creature fly to the branch of a nearby tree. She stifled a squeal of joy with her fist and then burst into the living room for a better view out her front bay window. The snow had all but melted by now, and the trees were dotted with bright, new leaves.

This called for celebration.

She showered and dressed quickly but took her time

walking down to Armitage Avenue, where she intended to stop for a leisurely coffee and some good conversation with Hailey. While it was still a bit chilly, the sun was warm on her skin, and that little bubble of hope was resurfacing. Things were on the up and up. That long, dark, lonely winter was finally behind her.

Mary spotted Hailey through the glass door, and happily let another couple exit before passing through. "Good morning!" she exclaimed.

"It sure seems that way," Hailey said. She glanced at her with suspicion. "Someone's cheerful this morning."

"Oh, well, the sun's out. Tomorrow's the first official day of spring. Who couldn't be happy about that?" Mary took her favorite seat near the espresso machine, happy to see that for a Saturday morning the café wasn't too crowded. Yet. Unlike Sunshine Creamery, Corner Beanery never struggled with a steady flow of traffic, regardless of the season.

"You sure that's all it is?" Hailey lifted an eyebrow suggestively.

"Of course," Mary said crossly. "The sun is out. That's good for my business." That was surely enough to warrant a good mood, even if she wasn't so sure that was the only thing lifting her spirits this morning.

Thursday night had been . . . unexpected. And enjoyable. Not just because of her time with Violet, but because of the look in Ben's eyes when he'd first poked his head around the door and come home.

"If you say so," Hailey shrugged. "It's just that from

the way you burst in here, I sort of thought maybe you'd met someone."

Mary's heart skipped a beat. "Met someone? Ha. Good one." Her voice felt strained and pitched and now Hailey was frowning with obvious doubt. "I mean, I would have told you if I'd met someone. Can't a girl be happy about something other than a man once in a while?"

"Absolutely," Hailey said firmly, and Mary suddenly wished she could feel as convinced as her friend. Instead, needles of doubt prickled the back of her mind, stirring up all those warm and fuzzy feelings that had percolated all day yesterday.

She couldn't stop replaying the moment when Ben had leaned in and taken the tiara from her head. She told herself it was nothing more than that, that she was misreading the situation, that God knew she had done that many times before, like when Jason said that instead of going out for New Year's Eve maybe they should stay in. She'd thought he meant stay in and have a cozy night on the couch, just the two of them. She didn't realize he meant stay in, and possibly, by themselves. Separately. *Alone.* But no, no, she wasn't misreading things with Ben. She'd seen the hooded look in his eyes, the way his mouth parted as his gaze drifted to her lips. And it was like every single nerve ending was on fire, and her mind was spinning and she wasn't even sure what she wanted anymore, or what she should do.

But she wasn't thinking about the kiss now. She hadn't

thought about that in at least ten minutes, not since she'd turned onto Halsted Street and seen that attractive married couple holding hands.

The kiss that never happened wasn't what she was so happy about. Of course it wasn't. It was the sunshine. The warmth. The relief that she'd gotten those pipes fixed. That soon all her troubles should be behind her. For a little while at least. She still had next winter to get through. Another long, harsh season with next to no income.

She frowned. She'd worry about that another day. No sense in getting ahead of herself.

"Oh no. I've ruined your mood." Hailey shook her head and reached into the glass case. "Here. A blueberry scone on the house. I insist."

Mary wasn't one to pass up an offer that good. "You know how much I love those blueberry scones."

"I do. And you know how much I love your blueberry pie ice cream."

Mary ordered a vanilla latte, her favorite, and broke off a corner of the scone. She hadn't seen Ben around the building since the other night, but chances were higher they'd bump into each other over the weekend. She pressed a hand to her stomach, pushing back the sudden burst of nerves. *He's just your neighbor*, she chastised herself. Only he was starting to feel like so much more than that.

"How are things going with your cousin?" she asked, hoping that by keeping the topic of conversation off herself, she'd stop thinking about things she shouldn't.

Her busy season was kicking off soon, after all. She needed to keep her priorities in order if she had any hope of keeping that business from going under. Now wasn't the time to be thinking of dating or romance.

And there was no way Ben was thinking of those things either.

Unless . . . was he? She closed her eyes, picturing his mouth so close to hers. Her pulse kicked.

"Claire seems okay." Hailey glanced over her shoulder into the back kitchen. "Between you and me, I'm a little worried about her. I don't think she's over her ex yet."

Mary took a sip of her coffee. "It takes time."

"Yes, it does, but it's hard to see her so down when the guy didn't deserve her at all." Hailey shook her head. "Why do women waste their time on men like this? You know the kind: emotionally unavailable, moody, hot one minute, cold the next? Hearing stuff like this, it makes me happy I'm single. Makes me *remember* why I'm single," she laughed bitterly.

Mary bit her lip, saying nothing. Hot one minute. Cold the next. It sounded familiar. Too familiar.

"Well," she said, clutching her paper cup. "I should probably get over to Sunshine and prep for the day." Her heart fluttered with sudden nerves. She might actually have a customer today. Maybe even more than one!

She said good-bye and left the café feeling a little more deflated than when she'd first arrived. The birds were chirping and the streets were filling with people ready to start their weekend. She had every reason to be looking forward to another spring and summer full of bustling activity, with a line out the door and sometimes even around the corner, the demand for her ice cream high and rewarding.

But all she could think about was her friend's subtle warning. And she started to wonder if Hailey was right—maybe she hadn't been excited this morning about the change of season.

Maybe she'd been hopeful about Ben's potential change of heart.

*

Ben looked out the window over the sink and onto the balcony of the apartment building next door. It was hardly a view, at least from this side of the building, but it was enough for him to see that all the snow had melted and the sun was shining brightly.

Violet was playing with her dolls in the corner of the living room. "How about we go to the park today?" he suggested, thinking that it might be nice for her to be outside and around other children for a bit. The fresh air would do them both some good, and it sure beat sitting around the apartment, even though he had made a few efforts to spruce up the place since Mary was over. Last night he'd even hung a few frames on the wall, and this morning before Violet awoke, he'd created a toy corner for her in the living room. It still felt temporary, and it was a far cry from his former house, but it was definitely less depressing. *One step at a time*, he reminded himself.

He packed a hat and gloves for Violet, just in case it was chilly, but there was a definite undertone of warmth in the air as they made their way over to the park. Ben eased onto a bench, watching as Violet climbed on the equipment, happy to entertain herself on the swings, easily making friends with some girls her age near the slide.

She was easing into the routine, feeling his shoulders relax. Slowly, somehow, she was adjusting. Ben just had to be careful, keep things positive, manage her disappointments, and not do anything crazy.

Like kiss his next-door neighbor.

He pulled back on the seat, hooking one leg over the other as he scanned the park, searching for a distraction. Most of the parents at the playground were women, and most seemed to know each other, standing in groups, deep in conversation, one eye drifting to their child every few seconds.

He looked across the playground to where a young couple was helping a toddler on the see-saw, and he felt something inside him begin to ache.

It was a longing, not for what he'd had with Dana, but for what he might have had, and maybe still could. If he let himself.

Abruptly, he pushed himself off the bench. There was no use going down that path. Nothing was ever simple, he'd learned. And he didn't need any more complications.

From somewhere in the distance there was the telltale ringing of a bell and the familiar song from the neighborhood ice cream truck. Ben counted the seconds, waiting for the request. Sure enough, Violet stopped pumping her legs on the swing and craned her neck to the sound.

She jumped off and bounded over to where he now stood alone, and feeling awkward, on the fringes of the playground.

"Can we go get ice cream?" Violet asked.

Ben held up a hand to shield the sun from his face. "I think it's looping the block, unless you want to try and chase it down?" It was something they always did when they heard the ice cream truck, a little game of theirs that admittedly sometimes ended with the fading of bells and tears of disappointment if they didn't discover the location in time.

"No, I meant ice cream at Sunshine Creamery. Mary's ice cream is way better than some boring old ice pop," Violet said, wrinkling her nose.

Ben hesitated, even though she had a point. Mary made damn good ice cream, better than she gave herself credit for. But it wasn't enough of a reason to keep dropping into her shop, not unless he wanted to foster something he wasn't so sure he should. A connection. With Mary. With Violet. With himself.

He looked into his daughter's eyes. She was so hopeful, and the weather was warm, and who was he kidding? His spirits rose at the mere thought of seeing Mary. And that was concerning.

*

For the first time in months, Sunshine Creamery had business. It was only midafternoon, and Mary had already served three families and an adorable teenage couple that almost made her believe in love again by the way they leaned across the table, sharing a hot fudge sundae, never taking their eyes off each other.

That was the kind of love she was searching for. That sweet, simple, confident love that made you feel all warm and fuzzy and happy inside. But did it exist? If it did, she was yet to find it. And she wasn't so sure it did.

She thought of Lila and Sam. Well, maybe it did, but the journey wasn't always an easy one. Nor did it come with a guarantee. And the next time around she needed that much.

She stopped and snorted at herself. What was she talking about? Next time. There would be no next time. Not unless she was sure that the next guy was different.

Her flavor of the day was coconut with toasted almonds and a shaving of rich, dark chocolate. It reminded her of the candy bar her grandfather had always enjoyed, usually sneaking one without her grandmother knowing, since she was forever going on about his cholesterol and the hazards of working in the sweets industry.

Mary snuck a spoonful of the cold, creamy concoction, rationalizing it by telling herself that she needed to test her recipes, and, satisfied, set some aside in a quart-sized container to take home later. She used to drop off the cardboard packaged treats to her sister or Hailey, until both women had all but begged her to stop tempting them, Lila pleading she would never fit into a wedding dress if she continued.

Mary didn't have that problem. There was no wedding dress. No nights of nudity in her near future. She doubted she would have a chance to even get to the beach this summer, so it wasn't like she needed to worry about bathing suits. Still, summer was coming, and with it came sundresses, and if recent experience had taught her anything, it was that you never knew who was on the other side of the door.

Speaking of . . . Her heart skipped a beat when she glanced at the window, and she almost knocked over an open container of cream when she saw Ben and Violet walking toward the shop.

She looked away, just in case they were passing by. A wave would be nothing short of awkward in that case. But, no, they were slowing down, and Ben was reaching for the handle, and . . .

She pushed her hair from her face and smoothed her blouse over her hips. "Ben! Violet!" she added, forcing herself to tear her eyes from that handsome face, that chiseled jaw, and that mouth that she'd inspected quite closely just a few nights before.

"You have customers today!" Violet announced loudly as soon as she walked into the shop, and two children at the back of the room turned to look up at her.

Ben frowned at Violet, but Mary could only laugh. "She's assertive," she pointed out, feeling a tingle as she and Ben shared a smile.

"And anything but subtle," Ben grinned. He tipped his head at his daughter. "The ice cream truck visited the playground today, but Violet insisted we come here instead."

Mary bristled with pleasure. "Well, that's quite an honor," she said, knowing she probably looked more flattered than she should be. "I always wanted to try something from the ice cream truck," she admitted. "But given that this was the family business, well, it didn't seem like a very loyal thing to do."

"I'm loyal, too," Violet said proudly. "You make the best ice cream, and I don't want to go anywhere else!"

Mary laughed again. "Loyalty is a good quality to have."

Ben's jaw tensed. "Sure is."

Mary felt her smile waver and she looked back at Violet and motioned her over to the counter. "We have some new flavors today. A few of the kids have chosen one I call Easter Basket Surprise."

Violet's eyes danced with excitement. "What's that?"

Mary motioned to the pastel-hued tub of ice cream through the glass. "You know those yummy little marshmallow candies they sell at this time of year? Well, I mix those up with vanilla ice cream, and a few secret ingredients, too."

Violet began nodding her head excitedly. "I want that! I want that, Daddy!"

Ben's smile had returned. "Why am I surprised?" he asked, chuckling as he studied the purple, blue, yellow, and pink ice cream that glistened with sugar crystals.

"Can I have a quarter for the jukebox?" Violet asked.

Ben fished out some coins. "Here are a few. And be careful not to spill your ice cream!" he called, as Violet grabbed her sundae bowl and hurried across the room.

He met Mary's gaze, shaking his head, but his eyes were inscrutable, and intense. She felt her breath still as her pulse sped up.

"It's nice seeing you here," she ventured, wondering if she'd overstepped. She watched Ben carefully, wondering if he'd mention the other night. Wondering if it had all been in her imagination.

"Well, Violet loves the ice cream and . . ." He drifted off, his expression turning serious. "Hey, what are you up to later?"

Mary opened her mouth, hoping something clever would pop out, but instead she was left with the unsettling feeling that she looked like a trout, blinking in confusion.

"Oh, a little of this, a little of that," she said casually, and then mentally cursed to herself. Okay, so she was a little . . . nervous around him. It didn't have to mean she liked him. It just meant . . .

Only she knew what it meant, and it meant she needed to tread carefully.

She scrubbed at some melted ice cream that had spilled on the counter, resisting the urge to ask why he'd asked, wondering if it was too late to do so, and hoping he would elaborate.

"We're having pizza later," he said.

She stopped scrubbing and cocked an eyebrow. "I'm curious. Is there ever a night when you don't have pizza?"

His smile was wry. "I'll have you know that I have an entire binder full of take-out menus. Sometimes, I have Thai."

She struggled not to laugh. "And are they arranged in alphabetical order or by cuisine?"

He rubbed a hand over his jaw, seeming amused. "Neither. But you've given me an idea."

She laughed and tossed the rag in the sink. She was just about to start on a batch of waffle cones when he said, "You could join us tonight. If you're free."

She looked up at him, her heart thudding. The smile had left his mouth and there was a decided edge to his gaze. If she didn't know better, she might think he was nervous.

"Violet would love it," he added quickly.

Oh. Mary felt like the air had been snapped out of her, and she wondered if he could see the embarrassment in her cheeks. So this was about Violet then. Not that she minded. The little girl was sweet, and Mary sensed that she needed some kindness right now.

"I don't close up until seven," she explained.

The tension seemed to leave Ben's face. "I'll place the order at six thirty then."

Mary gave him a small smile. "You have this takeout thing down pat, don't you?"

Ben shrugged. "It's one of the only things I do."

# Chapter Ten

Ben closed the pizza box lid and leaned back against the couch. Beside him, Mary sipped her wine, her hair falling loose, draping the side of her face from view. He had the urge to reach up, slip the auburn strands behind her ear, but he reached for his beer instead.

Down the hall, Violet was already asleep, even though she'd only been tucked in five minutes ago.

"It was all that sugar, I'm afraid," Mary said, smiling as Violet's snoring grew louder.

"More like all the excitement," Ben said. He paused, giving Mary a long look. "It helps, having you here. I'm afraid I'm a little useless when it comes to playing with dolls or wearing tutus."

"Oh, she loves you, though." Mary grinned. "It's sweet, watching the two of you together. It makes me wish I could remember more times like that with my own father."

Ben frowned. "What do you mean?"

"Oh, my parents died when I was young. I wasn't much older than Violet, really. My sister and I went to live with my grandparents after that. They're gone now, too."

"I'm sorry to hear it," Ben said, feeling the familiar weight of guilt. He took his family for granted sometimes, especially of late. Sometimes it was too easy to get lost in yourself, forget about how much worse it could be.

"It's okay," Mary said, reaching out to set her hand lightly on his arm before pulling it back again. "It happened a long time ago, and I have my sister, at least. We're very close." She tipped her head, her gaze roaming his face with interest. "What about you? Do you have any brothers or sisters?"

"A sister," Ben said a little begrudgingly. "Emma is younger than me by a few years."

Mary lifted an eyebrow. "Not a close relationship?"

Ben sighed. "She's a shrink. Sometimes I think she forgets I'm not one of her patients."

"Ah." Mary smiled as she finished the wine in her glass. "My sister can be that way too. Older. Wiser. Thinks she knows better." She shrugged and leaned in a touch, close enough for Ben to catch a hint of her flowery perfume. "Half the time she does, but don't tell her I said that."

Ben laughed. "My sister's been a little overbearing.

Since the divorce."

"Which was?"

"We separated about two years ago," Ben said. "Divorced shortly thereafter."

Mary jutted her lip, soaking in this information. "And you've been living here all this time?"

Ben glanced around the room. Even though he'd made more of an effort since Violet had moved in, it was still sparse, still lacking a lived-in feeling. He hated to think what it said about his state of mind. But then, he already knew. His sister had told him. Depressed, she'd said, tsking. A man who had given up.

"We have a house. *Had* a house," he corrected himself. "Dana, my ex, well, she's selling it."

"That must be strange," Mary said.

"Very," Ben agreed. It felt like a relief admitting that, without being analyzed or judged in the way that would inevitably follow opening up to his sister, or without the worried crease that always formed between his mother's and father's brows if he dared to betray an emotion other than complete happiness. "It's especially difficult because I oversaw the renovation of that house."

"Could you design another one?" Mary suggested.

Ben took a long sip of his drink and contemplated this. "I suppose I've never thought of it. An apartment suits my life better now. Maybe I'll buy a condo soon now that Violet's come to stay with me. There's been a lot of change lately, though. I'm not sure how much she can handle right now."

He looked over at Mary. Mary was a good change, he decided. A light in Violet's life. And, if he was being honest with himself, his own life, too.

"Do you ever look back on your life and wonder how the hell you got here?"

Mary laughed. "Every day." She shook her head. "When I think back on how eager I was to take over Sunshine, how optimistic I felt . . . It's hard to believe that was less than a year ago. I feel like a different person now. I guess reality does that to you."

"Dana and I met in college. I remember thinking that the world was wide open, that anything was possible. We were in love, young, and it never even crossed my mind that we'd be a statistic. Divorced. I never even considered it."

"I guess all anyone can do is hope for the best in life, or what's the alternative?" Mary shrugged. "Sometimes I ask myself why I did this, took on the ice cream parlor, put myself in this position. I've sacrificed so much. But if I'd never tried . . . Well, that doesn't seem like an option."

"It wasn't an option," Ben said. "But there's still a chance for you and for your grandfather's business. Don't quit yet."

"I don't want to quit," Mary said, frowning. "But I'm not sure I'll have much of a choice." She paused, studying him. "Is that how you felt?"

"I tried to make my marriage work," Ben said, knowing that was the truth. Looking back there was nothing he could have done differently. He couldn't control Dana. Couldn't make her someone she wasn't. "I was holding on for Violet's sake. I wanted her to have what I had. Two parents under one roof. Stability. It killed me to think of her being shuffled back and forth."

"Kids can bounce back from a lot," Mary said. "I did."

Ben considered her angle. "I know Violet's not the first kid to be in this position. I know it's not the end of the world. It's just not what I wanted for her. This . . ." He waved his hand over the apartment. "Sometimes it's hard not to wonder where it all went wrong. To pinpoint that exact moment when life went off course."

"You're a good dad, Ben," Mary said softly.

Ben swallowed hard. No one had ever said that to him, at least not from what he could recall. He'd spent so much time living with the guilt, the fallout from the divorce, replaying every step up until it, making sure his visits with Violet went well, that she had fun. And lately, trying to make up for yet another disappointment.

"Sometimes I feel like all I've ever done is fail her."

"I didn't have a traditional family," Mary pointed out. "But I never felt like I was missing out. I missed my parents, I still do," she admitted. "My grandparents, though . . . they gave me love. And it was enough in many ways."

Mary reached out and took his hand, giving it a small squeeze. He waited to see if she would let it go, but she left it there. It felt small, warm and soft. "We all just do the best we can. It's easy to be hard on ourselves, wonder what we could have done differently."

"And what do you have to feel guilty about?" he asked, genuinely curious.

"The ice cream parlor." She sighed and pulled her hand away to tuck her hair behind her ear. "I worry that I won't be able to keep it going. That I will have let my grandparents down."

"We're more alike than I first thought." He paused, then added, "Even with all your *little building initiatives*."

She gave him a playful swat, and a bolt of desire zipped through him. "I think you just misjudged me. Though, in fairness, I might have done the same."

His gaze drifted lazily over her pretty face. "Well then, it's a good thing we figured things out."

His eyes caught hers, just for a beat, and he heard her breath catch. Her eyes were soft, a warm cinnamon brown nearly the same color as her hair, and he felt something deep within him come to life.

His gaze fell to her lips, soft and rosy pink and so full and smooth, he could almost imagine their taste. He leaned in, feeling the temperature as he did, slowly, just in case she didn't want to, just in case he came to his senses and changed his mind. Only he wasn't thinking, not clearly anyway. No, he was just feeling, acting on his feelings, on this need that wouldn't go away, on the desire that he couldn't shake.

He kissed her softly, his lips brushing hers, and a surge of heat tore through him at the sensation. He kissed her again, lightly, and she opened her mouth to his, leaning in until she was close enough for him to reach out and touch. He wrapped an arm around her waist, sliding her body closer to his until the swell of her breasts were pressed up against his chest. Their kiss grew deeper, and he could feel the pounding of her heart against his body, the warmth of her skin and the honey scent of her hair. He kissed her long and hard, wanting to abandon himself to this moment, to think of nothing, but to just feel the taste of her mouth, the smooth curves of her body, the comfort of her touch.

Slowly, they pulled apart. Her lips curved into a slow, shy smile. Her lashes fluttered when she blinked. "That was nice," she said softly.

"It was," he said, his voice husky and low. He tensed. His bedroom was just a few feet away, but so was his daughter's. If she stayed much longer, looking at him from under the hood of her lashes like that, he wasn't sure he'd be able to hold back from wanting more. And he did want more. So much more.

"Are you free next Friday?" he asked, remembering the sleepover party Violet had been looking forward to since she brought home the invitation. "It might be nice to have an evening to ourselves. Just the two of us."

"I'm looking forward to it." She tipped her head toward the door. "I guess I should probably go."

Neither of them made any motion to move, and Ben fought the urge to kiss her again, knowing if he did, it could lead to more than it should . . . for tonight. Finally, she stood, and Ben resisted the disappointment he felt.

He'd see her Friday. And if he couldn't wait until then, he knew where to find her.

\*

Mary knew that she needed to put Friday out of her mind, almost as much as she needed to stop thinking about that kiss. But as the hours slowly ticked by on Sunday, she knew there was little chance of that.

Sunshine Creamery was busy all afternoon, and chances were it would just continue on that trend through the spring and summer. In many ways, it was as if these long, lonely, worrisome months had never happened at all. The hole in her ceiling had been patched, and now there was no evidence that it had ever even been ripped up. No one would have any idea that anything had happened here: that the pipes had burst, that she'd seen no income for three months. No one would be any wiser. No one other than her.

Something had to change, and she just wasn't sure what. But she couldn't continue on this path forever, working long shifts and making the ice cream, handling the books and the maintenance, without any help. Her grandparents had each other. And what did she have?

That little bubble returned to her stomach, but she just dug her metal scoop deeper into a batch of chocolate chip ice cream and smoothed it into a waffle cone before handing it over to a smiling boy with two missing front teeth.

She didn't have anyone, not technically speaking. *Not yet anyway*, she thought, allowing herself one more memory of that kiss.

Mary closed the shop at seven on the dot that evening, deciding not to stick around to clean up, but instead, to come in early the next day. Most Sundays, she had dinner with her sister and Sam. It was a standing invitation; the door was always open to her, and since her last break up, she'd been taking them up on the offer.

Unsure of what would happen if she ran into Ben so soon after the kiss and so many days away from their date, and not wanting to sit in her lonely apartment and worry about things like Sunshine Creamery and how she would handle next winter, or the credit card debt she'd accrued over the last few months, she grabbed her coat and walked east toward Lila and Sam's apartment. Lila always had a way of making her feel like a guest, and she knew it was a win-win for both of them. Lila liked to dote on her, and sometimes Mary liked to feel taken care of. Other people had mothers, aunts, spouses to fill their hearts. She had Lila.

And the ice cream parlor, she reminded herself firmly.

She was only three blocks from her sister's street when she saw him. Standing at the corner, his hand held in the air to hail a cab, it would have been so easy to pretend she hadn't seen him, kept walking. Her heart began to pound as she stared at him. He was just as tall as she'd remembered, with the same thick eyebrows and haircut, but then, people didn't change much in a few months, did they? No, Jason looked exactly the same now as he did the last time she'd seen him, the day before he'd abruptly ended their five-month relationship. In a one-line text.

She pursed her lips, recalling Jason's heartless suggestion that she "cross the friendship bridge" and, before she stopped to think things through, did the next thing closest to that and crossed the street.

He didn't notice as she approached, and with a loud and clear voice, a hint of feigned surprise in her tone, as if she wasn't quite sure it was him, because it had been that long and because she never really thought of him, she called out, "Jason?"

He dropped his hand, turning in confusion, but when his eyes found hers, they widened slightly. "Mary. Wow. Mary. I've . . . um, I've been meaning to call."

She put on her sweetest smile, pretending that her heart wasn't thudding, that this was easy for her, that she was over it. That she didn't wonder where she went wrong, that she hadn't questioned her choices. That she didn't sometimes sit in that empty storefront and wonder if she could have been sitting in Jason's apartment instead.

She knew he hadn't been meaning to call. It angered her that he could think she'd even want him to. Even if she had . . . once. "You were? Why?"

He gaped at her for a moment, and then ran his hand through his hair. She mentally rolled her eyes. He was a bad liar. Why hadn't she ever seen that before?

But then, she'd overlooked many of Jason's faults before. She'd seen what she wanted to see. The fun times, the suggestions of weekend getaways that she was never in a position to take. But when it got deep, when the conversation mattered, well, he stopped listening, didn't he?

"How are you?" he asked, even though he didn't seem to particularly care for a real answer.

"Good, very good," she said, nodding coldly. "I'm just leaving work now, actually."

Jason frowned. "Still making ice cream?"

She scowled at him, hearing the scorn in his voice, realizing it had always been there. It wasn't just that he hadn't supported her dream to keep her family business going, that he found her weekend and evening hours inconvenient, it was that he looked down on it, thought it somehow beneath him.

"Still *running* Sunshine Creamery," she clarified. She looked him up and down, feeling the distance that had somehow, naturally, come to her. He was handsome, objectively speaking, but she wasn't attracted to him anymore, she realized with a start. To be attracted to someone, you had to like them inside out, and she didn't like Jason very much after all.

A cab with glowing lights appeared down the street, and Mary jutted her chin toward it. "Grab it before someone else does."

"It was nice seeing you, Mary," Jason said.

"Yeah, real nice," Mary said, matching his polite tone. She turned her back and walked away, not waiting until he'd climbed into the cab, only she didn't continue on toward her sister's house. Somehow the thought of being in her apartment didn't feel so lonely, and somehow the thought of those bills and debts didn't feel so looming.

Her step felt lighter as the feelings that had weighed on her for months began to melt away, as quickly and surely as the long winter's snow. For months she'd wondered if she'd been at fault, if she'd made the wrong choices, prioritized the wrong things. Now, that doubt was over.

Jason wasn't the guy for her. Not in the end, and probably not even when they were together. She needed a guy who supported her dreams, not one who stomped on them. She needed someone who understood her choices. Someone who believed in the meaning of family.

And she knew one guy who most definitely did.

# Chapter Eleven

Mary eyed the clock on her nightstand. Ben was going to knock on her door in exactly twenty-two minutes for their date, and her sister was still sitting on her bed, lazily flicking through bridal magazines. Sam was going out for drinks with some guy friends, she'd told Mary when she spontaneously dropped by fifteen minutes ago, while Mary was still trying to catch her breath from her near sprint home.

"So, a Friday night to yourself, huh?" Mary stood anxiously in the entrance to her bedroom, craning her neck toward the front door in case Ben decided to stop by a little early. "Sounds like the perfect night for a good book and a bubble bath," Mary said, hoping her sister would take the hint.

Lila sighed, and then closed the magazine. "I had

another idea."

"Oh?" Mary eyed her closet door. She'd hoped to change and fix her makeup before eight o'clock, but at this rate, she'd be lucky to have time to even brush her hair.

Lila's eyes gleamed. "Let's order a pizza. With all the toppings. I've been on this wedding diet for so long, I've forgotten what carbs even taste like anymore."

Mary smiled weakly. She missed these nights alone with her sister. Back when they were roommates they'd had a routine, the comfort of each other's company. They'd go to the Farmer's Market in Lincoln Park every weekend when it was in season, spend their summer weekends reading on the warm sand sticking their toes in Lake Michigan's icy water. They'd eat dinner together, sitting on the little fire escape they'd turned into a makeshift balcony, and chat over wine. But Lila had Sam now, and Mary had Sunshine Creamery.

And tonight she had a date. One that started in—she glanced at the clock—nineteen minutes.

She eyed her sister, who was perched on the bed, patiently waiting for Mary's response. Mary felt her shoulders slump. There was no way around it. She was going to have to tell her sister about her plans.

"I actually have . . . a date tonight," she said. She closed her eyes, bracing herself. When she opened them again Lila was staring at her with a knowing smirk.

"A date? I knew all that talk about not needing a guy was just a defense mechanism."

"No," Mary insisted, growing cross. "It wasn't. I really would rather be alone than with another guy who is just going to blindside me, and dump me without warning."

She felt her pulse begin to flicker. Ben seemed nice, but was he different than the rest? She thought of the way he was with Violet, the tutus littered around his man cave of an apartment, the tenderness in his eyes when he spoke of her.

He was different, she told himself firmly. Otherwise, she wouldn't be risking her heart again.

"Well, this guy must be really special then."

"He is," Mary said defensively. "I mean, I think he is." She frowned.

"Where'd you meet him?" Lila asked as she crossed one long leg over the other.

Mary eyed the clock. Her sister was settling in for a long chat, but Mary was down to seventeen minutes.

"Just . . . around," she said vaguely as she walked over to her closet and flicked on the light. Around the building. Around the third floor. Yes, *around* would suffice.

She could feel the heat of Lila's gaze on her back. Her sister wasn't buying it, and why should she?

Mary pulled her favorite black dress from the hanger, remembered that she had worn it the first—and last—time she'd gone out to dinner Jason, and quickly put it back. She needed something fresh and new, nothing to taint this evening or remind her of the past.

"Just around?" Lila mused. "Wouldn't be . . . around the building, would it?"

Mary turned, flashing her eyes on her sister, who was struggling to compose herself. "Okay, fine. If you must know, the man I'm going out with tonight is Ben. The man across the hall."

"Mary!" Lila slapped a hand against the bed, the sound muted by the thick duvet cover. "I told you, he's no good!"

Mary pulled in a breath and counted to three as she crossed the room and pulled open her dresser drawers. Black pants and a slinky top. Perfect. She'd bring a cardigan in case she got chilly.

"I told you," she said, as she wiggled out of her work clothes. "He's—"

"Troubled." Lila's eyebrows rose. "I know."

"He's had a rough time lately. The divorce—"

"He's divorced!" Lila cried. "Mary, what are you doing?"

"I'm putting myself out there again." Mary's hands shook as she fastened her earrings. "I thought that's what you wanted."

"But he lives across the hall! You just moved in. If things don't work out, won't that be awkward?"

Mary swallowed hard. Her sister had a point. She usually did.

"Who said it won't work out?" she asked pertly, but she felt the familiar twinge of unease in her stomach. She glanced at the clock. Fifteen minutes now.

"I just don't want to see you get hurt again," Lila said. She shook her head, sighing with an air of disappointment. Mary stared at her, thinking of all the times she'd acted impulsively, all the times she'd messed something up and had gone running to her sister to help make things better. She thought of Sunshine Creamery, and how she'd relied on her sister to keep it open right after their grandfather had passed, how she'd been so sure this was what she wanted, that she'd be good at it, that she'd succeed.

"I know what I'm doing," she said, and left the room to go primp in the bathroom.

She closed the door behind her, her heart feeling heavy, but not because she didn't like fighting with her sister.

Because her sister was always right. And because she wasn't so sure she knew what she was doing at all.

*

Ben stood in front of the Italian bistro, completely silent, trying to understand what he was looking at. The tall glass windows were covered in brown paper, the light above the front door was dim, and the two signs taped to the inside glass indicated the restaurant had closed more than ten months ago.

Oh, wouldn't Emma have a field day with this.

"I guess it's been a while since I've been here." More like it had been a while since he'd been out at all, unless you counted kid-friendly activities as a healthy social life. "I loved this place. I thought you would too." He turned to Mary, whose brown eyes shone with amusement.

"I don't mind," Mary said with a shrug, and something in her demeanor told him she didn't, that it wasn't about an expensive meal, or candlelight, or a trendy scene. That she was here for him. For the right reason. That her priorities were in the right place.

"There's a sushi place around the corner," he suggested.

She raised her eyebrows. "It closed last summer. It's a frozen yogurt place now."

"Oh." He ran a hand over his jaw, his mind coming up blank. "You know, I actually put some thought into this," he said to her, lest there be any confusion.

"I know," she said lightly. "But I don't care where we go. I'd even be happy with . . . pizza."

He barked out a laugh. "You're kidding me."

"I like pizza," she said simply. "And I know you do, too. What do you say? My place?"

Ben grinned. "I say yes."

They stopped by the corner grocery store on their way back to the building to buy frozen pizza dough, fresh mozzarella, a variety of toppings, and a bottle of champagne.

"Classy," Mary laughed, as he added the bottle to their basket.

"Hey, it is our first date," he said, exploring the word on his tongue. A date. He hadn't been on a date since college. It felt foreign, strange, and almost natural all at once. Mary was easy to be with, casual with her conversation, familiar somehow.

"Well, in that case . . ." Mary plucked a box of chocolates from a shelf on their way to the check-out line. "Can't forget dessert."

"You mean your freezer isn't stocked with ice cream?"

Mary laughed. "Oh, it is. But even I get tired of it after a while. Shh." She held a finger to her mouth as she grew close to his ear, her breath light and warm on his skin, causing his skin to prickle with pleasure.

The brownstone they shared was just up the block, and Ben found himself looking at it with fresh eyes. It was no longer a symbol of failure, a depressing hovel he'd been reduced to. Now it was the place where Violet lived, where Mary lived, where good things had started to happen, where new possibilities began. For the first time, it felt like home.

It was strange to stand outside his own door instead of going inside as Mary turned the lock in her own door. He blinked as she turned on the light, trying to process what he was looking at. Mary's apartment was in the front of the house, his in the back, but despite the fact they shared a floor of the old house, he may as well have been in another world. Whereas his apartment looked cold and sterile, hers had a cozy, lived-in feeling. The long windows were lined with curtains, the couch was covered with a soft-looking throw blanket and colorful pillows, and she'd painted the walls a soft, creamy shade of blue, instead of the industrial white he'd never bothered to cover up in all this time.

He let out a low whistle. "This is really nice. I can only imagine what you think of my place," he added ruefully.

Mary gave him a pointed look. "If you saw my ex's apartment, you wouldn't feel so bad. He had plastic milk crates for a coffee table. I'm not sure he owned a second pair of sheets for his bed." She wrinkled her nose, and he laughed, but his curiosity grew along with something else...He didn't like the thought of Mary being with another man, spending time in his home, laughing at his jokes.

He wanted Mary to himself, he realized with a start. More than he had admitted.

"Do you mind me asking what happened?" he asked as he followed Mary into her bright and cheerful kitchen, so much different than his merely functional one.

Mary shrugged as she pulled two wineglasses from the cabinet. "Oh, he had a change of heart, I suppose. Or maybe his heart was never in it at all. I suppose I misread things."

Ben frowned. He could have said the same thing about himself and Dana. He'd always thought they wanted the same things, but maybe he'd never bothered to ask, or maybe he'd overlooked things from the start, seen what he wanted to see, believed in something that wasn't there.

He wouldn't be making that mistake again.

"How long were you together?"

"Not long. But . . ." Mary paused, as if considering how much she wanted to reveal. "It was long enough to think there could be more, you know? Sometimes it's the loss of hope that hurts the most."

He nodded silently. That made sense. Too much sense.

"I don't think about it too much now, though," Mary said with a small smile. "To be honest, I have bigger worries on my mind." She handed him a wine glass. "Sorry. I don't have any champagne flutes."

He shrugged away her concern and began unpacking the groceries from the bag. "You're still worried about the business?" he asked.

"It wasn't doing well when I took it over. I felt so confident I could make it work. I was so sure of myself!" She shook her head. "I guess fresh paint and some new tables don't make that much of a difference, after all. And I hadn't expected such a slow winter. At this rate, it won't last forever, but . . . I don't think I could bear the thought of it closing down. It would be like an entire chapter of my life, gone."

Ben felt his jaw tense. "I think I can relate."

Mary set a hand on his arm. "Oh, Ben, listen to me. Going on and on about an ice cream parlor, when you . . . Well, I'm being silly."

"Not at all," he said firmly. "But I know what you mean about starting a new chapter. For a long time, I couldn't imagine it, it didn't feel possible."

"And now?" Her lips curved into a shy smile with just

a hint of suggestion, and her eyes sparkled as they locked with his.

"Now I feel like anything is possible," he said, leaning in to brush her mouth with his. She kissed him back, slowly, softly, as if she were savoring the experience, making it last. He ran his hand through her hair, down the length of her neck, dropping his other arm to her waist to pull her close. Her body felt warm next to his as she reached her arms up around his neck, pressing the length of herself against his chest.

His groin stiffened with need and he pulled back. He wanted to take this slow, not rush through the night.

"I feel like I'm playing hooky," he admitted, thinking of his daughter at her sleepover party. "I've been so worried about Violet. Until lately," he admitted. He brushed a strand of hair behind Mary's ear, looking into her eyes. "You've made her smile again, Mary. Thank you for that."

Mary blushed at the compliment. "It's nothing."

"No," he corrected her firmly. "It's more than you realize. She's had a rough time lately. Too much change."

"I care about you, Ben. And about Violet." Her eyes were soft, searching.

"I know," Ben said, tearing his gaze from hers. He didn't want to dwell on hard times tonight. Those dark days were fading behind him.

He reached into the bag, found the bottle of chilled champagne. "Shall we?" Without waiting for an answer, he popped the cork, and Mary burst out laughing at the sound.

"What are we celebrating?" she asked when they'd clinked glasses.

"A new beginning," he said.

"I like the sound of that," Mary said, smiling.

\*

The pizza was a success, and Ben had even admitted that it was better than the take-out variety he ordered most nights. "We used to do this when I was younger," Mary explained, as they carried their dishes to the sink. "Gramps loved interacting with us in the kitchen."

"So it extended beyond ice cream, then," Ben said.

Mary nodded. "They must have been tired, looking back on it. My sister and I could be a handful, I'm sure, but they never made us feel unwelcome or that we were a burden. They were just happy to have us. And we were happy to have them," she added, with a sad smile. "It was the one good thing to come out of a terrible situation."

"I guess we all make the most with what we're handed," Ben said, his brow pinching in thought. "As much as I hate what my ex did to Violet, I'll admit that I'm happy to have her with me."

"Silver linings," Mary mused. They were standing very close, she realized, and neither of them was showing any sign of reaching for that box of chocolates that had looked so delicious just a couple hours ago at the store.

"Are you always this much of an optimist?" Ben asked.

She looked up at him in surprise. "I suppose I used to be . . ." She frowned a little. "Sometimes it's not so easy to see the bright side, though."

"I feel like I could learn a thing or two from you," Ben said. He gave a small shrug. "Maybe I already have."

Mary watched as Ben set down his glass and brought his arms around her waist, her heart beginning to beat a little faster at the proximity. "I've been wanting to kiss you all week," he murmured, leaning in to brush his mouth to hers.

Mary grinned into the crook of his neck. "I was surprised I didn't run into you at all." But then, given her work hours, she wasn't entirely. She'd been putting in extra time at Sunshine, especially now that she had customers again, but even then, it wouldn't be enough to offset the slump from the past few months.

She closed her eyes. No point in thinking about that tonight. Tonight she would think about Ben, that slow smile, the musk coming off his warm skin, the way her body tingled when he pulled her a little closer.

"I'm sort of happy we didn't, actually." Ben's voice was low and smooth. "It added to the anticipation."

She pressed a hand against his chest, feeling the rhythmic beat under her fingertips, the warmth of his skin through his shirt. She looked up into his eyes. His lips were parted as he leaned into her, and she accepted him freely, her mouth opening to his, his kiss slow and deep, full of endless unspoken promises.

His fingers looped under the hem of her shirt, swirling

a soft pattern on her skin. She pressed herself closer against him as the heat of his fingers warmed her skin, the sensation of his touch sending bolts of heat through her body, making her ache for more.

Slowly, without a word, they moved down the hall and into the bedroom, Ben's hands wrapped around her waist from behind, his mouth teasing her earlobe, her neck. She turned to face him, and his mouth found hers as he pushed open the door, guiding her back onto her bed. She reached up, running a hand over the spread of his shoulders, reaching lower, up under his shirt, feeling the warmth of his skin under her fingertips.

Breaking their kiss, he trailed his mouth down her neck, and lower, as his hands slowly pulled her blouse off. She freed his shirt, one button at a time, needing to feel the smooth plane of his chest against her skin. His hands grazed her breasts over the lace of her bra, and she pulled in a sharp breath, her entire body stiffening in anticipation of his touch, and she eased into the pleasure as he slowly unhooked the clasp and teased her with his fingers, and then, his mouth.

She closed her eyes to savor the sensation, the feel of his body on hers, the rhythm of his heartbeat, the heat of his breath, soft in her ear. She opened herself to him, getting lost in the moment, sensing a change in herself, in him, as his kiss intensified. And for the first time in weeks she didn't want to worry about tomorrow, or think about the past. All she wanted to experience was tonight.

# Chapter Twelve

Mary woke up to a stream of sunlight poking through her curtains and the heavy weight of Ben's arm reassuringly tight across her waist. She smiled into her pillow and nestled a little closer to his chest. He roused against her, nestling his nose into the nape of her neck, his breath warm on her skin, the gentle rise and fall of his body so close to hers lulling her back into sleepiness.

Slowly, his hand came up around her breast, caressing it slowly as he began trailing soft kisses on her neck, her earlobe . . . She turned to face him and his mouth found hers before she could even say good morning. He tasted familiar and felt so right. Mary pulled him close, savoring the way his skin felt against hers, wishing they could stay like this all day, even though she knew they couldn't.

She had to go to work today. And Ben was picking up

Violet this morning from her sleepover.

Reluctantly, she pulled back from the kiss, and propped herself up on an elbow. "I could stay like this all day," she said.

Ben reached up and brushed her hair from her face. "Why don't you come to the zoo with us today? Violet would love to have you there."

Mary grimaced. "I have to work."

A shadow fell over Ben's face. "Of course. I don't know what I was thinking." He pushed himself up to a sitting position and reached for his undershirt that had fallen on the floor.

Mary watched with growing dread as he slipped it over his head, covering the smooth plane of his stomach, as if finalizing the end of their time together for the day.

"I could stop by later," she hedged. "Maybe we could have a late dinner?"

Ben shook his head. "I promised Violet we'd do something special today, and she had her heart set on this diner near the park after the zoo. You can join us there."

"Except that I probably wouldn't get there until after eight." Mary felt the pull of disappointment in her chest. It was the same way she'd felt when Jason had suggested a ski weekend in December and she'd had to say no. There was no one else to handle Sunshine Creamery. If she didn't show up, it didn't open. And somehow that didn't feel fair. To Lila. To her grandparents. Or to herself.

She wanted the family business to be a success. And that meant sacrificing other things.

But that same worried thought nagged her quietly. Was she sacrificing too much? And for what end? If Sunshine Creamery closed down, it would all be for nothing. It was another reason she had to fight to make it work. To make everyone's input worthwhile.

She eyed Ben nervously as she slipped on jeans and shirt, feeling him slip away, the first prickle of a problem in their new relationship.

"I'm hoping to get some help soon," she said aloud. It was true, but it was also a pipe dream at the moment. She didn't even feel optimistic by voicing it. Somehow it just felt more unrealistic than ever.

Who was she kidding? Sunshine Creamery was in the red. It was in the red when her grandfather had died and asked her to keep it going. Last summer had been promising, but a few months of strong activity was hardly enough to sustain a business.

And she would rather go to the zoo today with Ben and Violet. Instead she had to go to work.

"Do you ever take time off?" Ben asked. His tone was conversational, but the mere question put Mary on edge.

"Technically, I can. I mean, I own the place. But . . ." She bit her lip, considering it, just like she'd considered it back when Jason had proposed that weekend trip. Every little bit counted, and that was just the problem. Closing shop for a day meant a loss of sales for that time. And she couldn't afford to lose any more sales. Just like she couldn't afford someone to cover the counter once in a while. "I'm not exactly in a position to take a day off at the moment," she finished.

Ben's expression seemed to turn to one of concern. "I didn't mean to upset you," he said.

Mary smiled at his kindness. She was getting jumpy, fretting over nothing. Ben wasn't Jason. Ben understood what Sunshine meant to her, and why. She was just projecting her own insecurities, worrying about things that weren't even there.

"You didn't. It's just hard. The business . . . I didn't stop to consider what an undertaking it would be."

"Is it worth it?" Ben asked. "The sacrifice?"

Mary frowned, wondering if he meant the sacrifice of her money, or of her time. "Of course it is," she said firmly. And it was. It had to be.

She walked to the edge of the bedroom and motioned to the bathroom. "I have a spare toothbrush in there somewhere."

Ben just shrugged. "I'll just walk across the hall."

"Oh. Right. Of course." It made sense, she told herself. After all, why use her bathroom when his own was a mere doorway away? "I'm sorry I can't come to the zoo today," she said, hoping he would sense the regret in her voice.

She blinked out the window. April was just a few days away. The sun was shining, the birds were chirping, and spring was starting to bloom. She felt a strange sadness, the way she did last year when she'd missed her weekends at the lake, the sand on her toes, a good book on her lap.

"Don't worry about it," Ben said, but she detected a change in his demeanor. His jaw seemed squared again, his eyes distant.

"Hey," she said, coming to slip her arms around his waist. She looked up into his muddy blue eyes. "What about brunch tomorrow? I make a mean stack of pancakes." She didn't open until noon on Sundays. Surely he would see that she was trying. That spending time with him was important to her.

His smile returned. "I can't think of a better way to start my morning. Well, other than this." He bent down, his mouth fusing with hers for a beat, long enough to send shots of heat down the length of her thighs, tightening in her abdomen. She pressed herself to him, feeling the warm, sleepy heat from his skin, wishing they could just hop back into bed, go for a walk, and have a long, leisurely coffee before she went to work.

But he had Violet to attend to, and children needed time and attention. Two things she wasn't so sure she was in a position to give, despite her desire to offer both.

She wondered if he sensed that, too.

\*

It was a beautiful spring day, and the perfect afternoon for a trip to the Lincoln Park Zoo. Violet held Ben's hand the entire walk there, skipping alongside him as she recanted the details from last night's sleepover party, right down to what they ate, what color pajamas everyone wore, and how much more fun it was to sleep in a sleeping bag than a bed.

"I can't wait to tell Mommy," she said, when she'd finally taken a breath.

Ben nodded slowly. There was little he could say in response. Technically, Dana had promised to phone at least every Sunday, but given her track record, he didn't want to remind Violet of this. He wasn't prepared to set his child up for potential disappointment. All he wanted to do was shield her from it.

They stopped for popcorn as soon as they entered the zoo, and they shared it as they walked along the path, stopping to admire the lion, who Violet was convinced had waved a paw at her. Violet always had the tendency to want to feed the animals, and Ben had to keep stopping her from tossing them a few kernels of the popcorn, ignoring her protests that they would probably enjoy the snack, because who didn't love popcorn?

In the distance, the Chicago skyline was clear, and all around them were couples pushing baby strollers, parents wrangling toddlers that giggled as they ran, and families out to enjoy the first warm weekend of the year.

Ben felt a weight in his chest as he slid his sunglasses onto his face, the steady reminder of everything he'd always wanted, everything he'd thought he'd had. He pushed the heaviness aside as he saw Violet's face light up when she spotted the flamingos, dancing around the edge of the lily pond. Their pink feathers never ceased to delight her, but there was something else, Ben noticed, something deeper. She was happy. It had been almost four weeks since Violet had come to stay with him. The change had been so gradual, so slow to evolve that he'd almost stopped believing it would ever happen. But he could see it now, as clear as the sun over their heads. His daughter was smiling in that carefree way children should. The way he'd always wanted her to be.

"What do you say we get some ice cream?" he asked, taking her by the hand after they'd looped through the zoo once.

"It won't be as good as Mary's ice cream," Violet warned.

Ben laughed. "No, it won't. But I don't mind this once."

They selected pre-packaged ice cream bars from the pavilion, and found a table in the sun to enjoy them. "I wish Mary could have come with us," Violet mused, as she bit into her strawberry-flavored bar.

Ben peeled back the wrapper on his ice cream sandwich, mulling over Violet's words. It would have been nice to have Mary with them. Very nice. But he couldn't overlook the fact that he was enjoying a day with Violet, just the two of them. Her bounce had returned to her step, and her eyes shone with delight. This was the kind of day they needed. It was a positive step, and one that gave him hope that things would only continue to get better.

Sometimes he worried what would happen if Dana decided to suddenly return, the impact it would have on Violet, on himself. Would she expect to uproot Violet again? And would Violet want to go live with her mother?

But then he remembered that Dana had decided to sell the house. That she had made no mention of returning any time soon. There was no doubt in six months or a year she'd be back, expecting a few gifts to make up for her absence, for things to gradually go back to normal. But this was the new normal. Him. Violet. He'd fight hard to ensure that. His daughter had experienced enough change for now.

"You like Mary, don't you?" Violet asked, her eyes focused on her ice cream bar, which was quickly melting all over her hands.

Ben leaned across the table to wipe her mouth with a napkin. "I do," he said. "Do you?" But he already knew the answer to that.

"I *love* Mary!" Violet corrected, smiling broadly. Just as quickly, a little wrinkle appeared between her eyebrows. "She's not going to leave us too, will she, Daddy?"

Ben opened his mouth to reassure Violet and then stopped. He couldn't make a promise he wasn't in control to keep. And no matter what he said or what he believed, there was always a chance that things wouldn't work out, that Mary would leave, and that Violet's heart would be broken. Again. That her world would stop making sense. That she'd lose the ability to count on anyone, to trust.

"Is she your girlfriend now?" Violet asked, not waiting for a response. "Isabelle's daddy has a new girlfriend. She buys Isabelle presents and lets her wear her lipstick!"

Ben's smile felt brittle as his mind began to race. He'd been planning on telling Violet that yes, Mary was his girlfriend now, that they'd be spending time together, holding hands, being affectionate. But now . . . Now all he could think about was the risk he was taking, at Violet's expense, not just his own.

"She's just a friend, honey," he said firmly, taking the last bite of his snack. "Our next-door neighbor."

He stood up and tossed his wrapper in the trash and jammed his hands into his pockets, turning his back to that blinding sun.

She couldn't be anything more than that. And shame on him for thinking she ever could.

\*

The next morning, Mary set the stack of pancakes on the table and eyed Ben carefully as she took her seat next to him. She'd thought it would be fun to have their brunch outside, maybe on a picnic blanket in the park, but as luck would have it, the first rainfall of the spring had started overnight, and it hadn't stopped all day.

Mary suppressed a sigh. Chances were she wouldn't have many customers today. She struggled with the thought of going into the shop at all, when she could be spending her time here, with Ben and Violet.

She glanced at Ben again. He'd been very quiet all morning, since Violet first came bounding across the hall, showing off her fruit salad. Mary had hovered in the doorway, waiting for Ben's lead, but he hadn't kissed her as she'd hoped.

*He has a child*, she reminded herself for the fifth time since they'd arrived. He probably wanted to take it slow. There would be time for displays of affection later, when they were alone.

"These are the best pancakes I ever ate!" Violet exclaimed happily, and Mary beamed at the compliment. "Don't you think so, Daddy?"

Mary noticed that Ben hadn't eaten much, and his coffee mug was still full. "Everything okay?" she asked quietly, as Violet doused her next pancake in syrup.

"We can talk it about it after," he replied, and Mary felt the cold, icy grip of fear knot her stomach.

So there was something wrong, then. She'd sensed it. But what? Why?

She struggled to finish her own plate, and was relieved when Ben finally suggested that Violet could be excused from the table to play.

"I'll just leave both of our front doors open," he said, glancing at her to confirm that this was okay.

Violet thought it was a brilliant idea. She skipped across the hall to play, and then poked her head back to look across the hall. "It's like one big house that we all share together!" she cried.

Mary felt her heart begin to tug, but when she met Ben's eyes, she saw that he wasn't smiling. Instead, his jaw was tight, his gaze distant, his brow pinched.

"Okay," she said in a voice soft enough that Violet wouldn't be able to hear, even if she grew curious. "What's going on?"

"Nothing's going on," Ben said, shaking his head. He blinked at the floor a few times, as if contemplating something.

"Well, something is clearly up," Mary insisted. "We had this brunch planned, and then you barely spoke to me the entire time you were here."

"I'm just . . . worried." Ben briefly met her gaze. "About Violet."

Mary felt a flicker of relief. He was worried about his daughter. She could handle that. She almost laughed at herself, at how silly she'd been, worried that something had changed between them, that Ben had had a change of heart.

"Did something happen?" she asked, feeling a bit of concern herself. "She seemed in good spirits."

"She is in good spirits. That's just the problem." Ben blew out a long breath, raked his hands through his hair. It was sticking out in various directions, and Mary reached out to fondly pat it down. She felt him stiffen under her touch; saw the pulse in his jaw, the flash in his eyes.

"Something is going on," she said firmly. Her heart was hammering. "Just say it, Ben."

Ben eyed the open door, and on instinct, Mary did the same. But Violet was already in her room, having an imaginary pancake breakfast with her dolls. Mary smiled sadly at the sound of her little voice, muffled by the distance.

Ben turned back to her. There was a sadness in his eyes she hadn't seen since that first day he and Violet had come into Sunshine Creamery. "I just think this is all moving too fast. Violet just came to stay with me, her mother upped and left her. It's a lot of change. Too much change."

Mary swallowed the lump that had formed in her throat and willed herself not to cry. She'd known this could happen, that it was the risk she was taking, but deep down she'd thought this time it would be different. That Ben was different.

She stared at his squared jaw, the flat look in his eye. He was hard again, distant, the stranger across the hall putting up walls.

"You know I would never do anything to hurt Violet," she said. *Or you*, she thought quietly to herself. Clearly, the same couldn't be said for him.

"Do I?" Ben asked. He shook his head. "See, that's the thing, Mary. We can't guarantee this will work out."

"I was willing to try." She fought the urge to take a step toward him, to put a hand on his arm, to reassure him as much as herself.

"If it was just me, it might be different." Ben paused,

his eyes locking hers, and for a moment she thought he was thinking it over, calming himself down. But then she saw that muddy shadow return, and she knew it was no use. "She's my daughter, Mary. I don't expect you to understand, but I have to do what I think is in her best interest."

"And this is for the best?" Mary clarified, crossing her trembling arms across her chest. "Ending things?"

"Before they get too serious . . ." Ben nodded. "Yes."

"Well then," Mary huffed. "I'm not going to try to change your mind, Ben. You've made your decision and I respect it. I suppose we have nothing left to say."

"Mary—" His voice was pleading, his eyes pained. "You have to understand."

Mary felt her heart soften even though it was breaking. "I understand," she said, holding back her tears. She understood more than she wished she did.

Ben was a good man. A man who loved his daughter. Who wanted to protect her. His heart was in the right place, even if it wasn't with her.

# Chapter Thirteen

The next Saturday morning, Mary sat in Lila's bedroom, trying to keep the tears in her eyes from falling as she stared at the beautiful ivory wedding gown that grazed the polished wood floor. They'd admired it for so many years when they were younger, but now, seeing it after all this time, knowing its significance, it somehow looked more beautiful than it did in her memory.

"Oh, Lila," she breathed, blinking hard. "It's . . . stunning."

Lila turned to inspect her reflection from the back. "You don't think it's too old fashioned?" She smoothed her hands over the satin A-line skirt, which was a pretty contrast to lace bodice.

Mary shook her head adamantly. "Absolutely not. It's classic. Elegant. It's . . . you." She gave a watery smile, not sure if the tears were out of guilt, or love, or the loss of something deeper than the past. The loss of hope for the future. It had always been what kept her going. No matter how dark the times, or how hard the struggle, she'd always believed that somehow, if she kept going, kept fighting, and didn't give up, that in the end things would have a way of working out.

Now, she wasn't so sure.

She plucked a tissue from the box on Lila's bedside table and dabbed her eyes. There was no use resisting it—the tears were flowing, hot and thick down her cheeks.

"Mary, what is it?" The heavy fabric of the dress swooshed as Lila crossed the room to sit on the edge of her bed. She rested a concerned hand on Mary's back, which only made Mary cry harder.

"It's . . . everything. My life . . . It's a mess. And now I'm going to have to move!" she cried, and then began sobbing into her tissue.

"Move?" Lila's tone was quizzical, but all at once she seemed to understand. "Mary," she warned. "This isn't because of—"

"Ben!" Mary tossed her hands in the air. "You were right about him, Lila. Of course you were right." She shook her head bitterly. Lila had her life tied up with a neat little bow. She had a beautiful apartment with a view of Lincoln Park. She had a gorgeous, doting fiancé whom she was madly in love with and quite possibly always had been. She was wearing their mother's wedding dress. She and Sam had more business than they could handle at their advertising agency.

While Mary . . . Mary thought she could handle it all on her own. So much for that.

"What happened?" Lila asked, patiently folding her hands in her lap.

Mary gave an abbreviated version of the story, starting with the first day that Ben and Violet had stopped into Sunshine Creamery. It felt like so long ago. She thought of the sweet little girl with the big blue eyes. Would Ben expect her to keep her distance from Violet now? To just be the friendly neighbor-lady who handed out candy at Halloween and said hello in the hall? She couldn't bear it. No more than she could bear the thought of occasionally running into Ben as he went down to collect his pizza, pretending that nothing more had ever developed between them, that no connection had been made. That they were just friendly neighbors.

"The saddest part of it all is that I don't even blame Ben for breaking things off. He did it from a good place. He was just trying to protect his daughter."

"From you?" Lila pursed her lips in disapproval.

"He doesn't want Violet to be disappointed again by another woman who can't give her everything she needs." Mary rolled the tissue in her hands. "She needs someone who is present, available. Not just someone who would love her."

"But you're present and available," Lila said.

"No," Mary corrected her. "I work every weekend.

Long hours," she pointed out. "I'm starting to wonder why I bother," she muttered, as the tears filled her eyes again.

"What do you mean?" Lila's voice was sharp.

Mary sighed. "Sunshine Creamery isn't as successful as I'd hoped."

"Well, it's always been a little slower in the winter," Lila pointed out.

"Yes, but I hadn't realized just how slow." She gave her sister a long look. "I'm starting to understand why the place was in the red when we inherited it."

"I always assumed the warm weather season sales made up for the loss. I sort of thought that Gramps was happy for a little downtime around the holidays." Lila frowned.

"I thought so, too," Mary admitted. "But that building is old. It's just one thing after another. I've started to ask myself if this is worth it. What I'm doing."

"What you're doing is fulfilling your dream," Lila said firmly. "You always loved that place more than I did. You were determined to take it over when Gramps passed away."

"True," Mary said begrudgingly. "But Gram and Gramps had each other. It's different doing it all on my own. I'm not really sure I can turn this around."

"The first question is whether you want to make it work," Lila said.

Mary looked at her sister as if she were crazy. "Of course I want to make it work, Lila! That's why I've worked so hard to keep it going all along."

A hint of a smile curved Lila's mouth. "Just checking. The next step is to think outside the box."

"I've tried that," Mary groaned. "I added all those new flavors! And people do like them!"

"I know they do." Lila tapped her lip in thought. "We'll turn the place around. I just wish you'd come to me sooner."

"I can't take any more of your money," Mary said, already preparing to stand. It was a mistake to open up to Lila, to worry her, to make this her sister's problem.

"Oh, I'm not offering any money," Lila told her casually. "I'm offering up something better. You, me, and Sam are going to sit down together and figure out how to rebrand Sunshine Creamery. You may be running things all on your own, but it's a family business, and we're your family."

That they were, and Mary couldn't have asked for more. She felt her spirits begin to lift as she considered an idea. "There was one thing I thought of. Well, actually it was Ben's daughter who made me think of that."

Lila looked at her with interest. "Back to Ben again, are we?"

"He's not a bad person," Mary said, feeling the need to rise to his defense. He just wasn't the guy for her.

\*

Ben knew it was his sister by the sharp rap at the door.

Emma wasn't one for pleasantries, never had been. She was brisk and matter-of-fact; something that fit her well in her professional environment, but not always in her relationships.

Ben smiled to himself as he crossed the living room to let her in. For someone who never stopped giving him advice, she could use a dose of her own. But then, the few times he'd dared to point this out, she'd made it clear that she was happy being alone, whereas he was not.

He pulled in a breath. Maybe she was right.

"How'd you get into the building?" he inquired once he'd firmly closed the door behind her. His heart still pounded after glancing out into the hallway, even though it was early afternoon and Mary was probably at work. A week had passed since their horrible brunch, and he still hadn't seen her. He didn't know whether to be relieved or disappointed by that. He missed her smile. Missed the way he felt when he was around her. But seeing her would only be complicated, and he still couldn't push out the image of her face when he'd let her down. The hurt in her eyes, the resignation in her words. He didn't know what he'd been expecting. But not that.

"One of your neighbors let me in," Emma replied. She dropped casually onto his couch and looked around the room, her nose wrinkling in overt disapproval. "Still haven't done anything to spruce things up, I see."

"What? Yes, I have!" Ben strode to the far wall and jabbed at the sole framed print. "What do you call that?"

Emma just gave him a pitying look. "Your shirt's all

rumpled. You slept in it, didn't you?"

Ben glanced down at his T-shirt, tried to smooth out some wrinkles with his palm. "So what if I did?"

His sister gave him a knowing look. "How's the pretty girl across the hall these days?"

"Mary?" Ben shrugged, hoping his body language passed as casual, but he felt tense and anxious just saying her name. "Fine, I guess."

Emma didn't look convinced. "Still seeing her?"

"Oh, now, I was never seeing her. She's my neighbor, and—"

"And you blew it." Emma rolled her eyes to the ceiling.

Ben drew a fist at his side. It was only late morning, but he felt like he could go for a beer. Or something harder. Something to take the edge off. Being with his sister was like being on trial. She meant well, but sometimes he wished he just had a sister who was happy to whine about her own life for a change.

"How do you know I blew it?" he asked, taking the armchair in the corner of the room.

"It's obvious, isn't it?" She blinked at him, her blue eyes wide. "Last time I saw you, you were so happy, so lighthearted. I'd go so far as to say you were downright cheerful."

"Well, that was Violet's birthday—"

She didn't let him finish. "And now . . . well, look at you." Her eyes turned hooded as her mouth pinched.

"You're back to sleeping on the couch with the television blaring all night, wearing the same clothes for days on end. I bet you've eaten pizza every night for at least five evenings in a row."

"Violet lives with me now. Last night we had pasta." He held her stare, but he knew it was no use. He would have ordered that pizza, and Emma knew it.

Emma dropped back against the sole throw pillow he had come away with in the divorce. He knew he could have fought for more, but he didn't care. It wasn't about where he lived or what he had.

"So what happened?" She tapped her fingers against the leather armrest. Ben watched her red nail polish move up and down, and knew that nothing he said was going to make her stop, or leave, or go find Violet in her room, which was her sole pretense for stopping over in the first place.

"There's nothing to tell, really," he finally said. "I like her. She's a sweet girl. A good person. But it's not fair to Violet for me to get involved with anyone right now."

Emma's eyebrow shot up. "But it's fair to Violet to see her father alone, and clearly unhappy being so? Admit it, Ben, you like being in a relationship. There's nothing wrong with that."

Ben's back teeth grazed together. "Violet needs my full attention now. She's been through a lot. She doesn't need to go through any more disappointment."

"And who said there would be another disappointment?" Emma countered.

"Is this how you speak to all your clients?" Ben replied.

"They're patients, not clients. And it's working, isn't it?" Emma winked.

"No," Ben shot back, but he knew that wasn't the truth. Emma had a point. It might be different with Mary. But *might* was a very big word.

"I'm not willing to take that kind of gamble," Ben said.

"So you're willing to spend the rest of your life alone?"

"I didn't say that," Ben shot back.

"But that's the choice you have," Emma said, her expression remaining strangely neutral.

*She's good*, Ben thought, with only a twinge of annoyance. "I don't have a choice," he said firmly.

"Ah, but you do. You always have a choice." Emma made a grand gesture of shrugging, indicating that it was his life, that he was a lost cause, that she'd given up on him. Just like a part of him had given up on himself. She pushed herself up from the couch and slowly made her way to the back hallway.

Ben tented his fingers, told himself to forget what she'd said, that she was stirring him up, that she was just being overly concerned like always. Only this time she'd hit a nerve.

"And what happens if it doesn't work out?"

She stopped with her hand on the wall and gave him a small smile. "And what happens if it does? You deserve happiness, Ben. Just like Violet."

Ben sat in the chair and listened to his sister and daughter play tea party in the purple bedroom he'd set up for Violet all those years ago. He smiled at their laughter, chuckled at the way Violet directed Emma through the ritual, even reprimanding her at one point for reaching for the fake sugar bowl instead of waiting to be served. And he thought of the one other person who had sat down in this very apartment, donned a tiara, and filled his daughter's world with imagination and hope.

And he thought of how different this past week had been when the sweet possibility of her stopping by no longer existed.

He swallowed hard, pushed himself out of his chair, and cursed to himself when he considered the triumphant look in his sister's eyes.

It was worth it. Some things were.

"I'm running out," he said, pausing in the doorway to Violet's room. "Mind babysitting for a bit?"

"Tell Mary I said hello," said Emma, before reaching for her plastic teacup.

\*

Mary stood behind the counter of Sunshine Creamery and stared into the empty storefront. The rain was coming down harder now, pelting the windows, and darkening the sky. Shadows danced on the walls, but other than that, the ice cream parlor hadn't seen any activity all day.

*Admit it*, she told herself. *You won't see a customer in here all day. You're wasting your time. You could be home with a good book.*

She glanced at Gramps's photo on the wall, her stomach knotting. She'd made a promise to him, a promise to keep this place going, and she'd given it her all. Her sister was right; she couldn't have done more if she'd tried. Maybe it was time to say good-bye to the old place, to let it go, to keep it only in memory, or maybe together with Lila and Sam, they would think of one last brilliant way to save it.

The ice cream truck idea had come to her that wonderful afternoon when Ben and Violet had stopped by. Was it worth pursuing though? Lila thought so. They'd talk with Sam, come up with a plan, and crunch some numbers.

She should have gone to her sister earlier. There was no use struggling on your own when people who cared about you and were willing to be on your team were there, if you were willing to let them in.

Mary sighed and brought a ruffle-edged bowl from the stack she kept on the counter. She considered her options, and decided that today was a Triple Truffle kind of moment. Nothing like chocolate ice cream with chunks of fudgy brownies and chocolate chunks to lift a mood. Or, maybe, soothe a broken heart.

She gave herself an extra large scoop and came around the counter to sit on a stool, turning her back to the windows. She wanted to face the shop, to listen to the old jukebox, to imagine that her grandfather was just in the backroom, that she could enjoy this shop without the worries she now associated with it.

The ice cream tasted just the way it had when Gramps made it. She'd treasured those recipes. She still did. At least they would carry on, even if this building didn't.

She was just finishing scraping the last bit of ice cream from her bowl when the bell above the door jingled.

She jumped, then reddened, feeling sly and underhanded, eating on the job, and guiltily turned to face the customer, for once hoping it was just her sister, and not someone who contributed to the till.

But it wasn't a customer. And it wasn't her sister, either.

It was Ben. Ben, with soaking wet hair and hesitant grin, looking more adorable than ever. For a moment she forgot that she was holding the ice cream cup and spoon, that her lips felt sticky with chocolate, and that he had broken things off with her last weekend. Her heart began to flutter and all at once the room felt brighter, despite the gloomy weather.

But just as quickly she remembered. She tensed and set the spoon on the counter next to the bowl. "What are you doing here?"

He frowned at her sharp tone, but she didn't apologize. He'd hurt her. Whatever his motives, however well his intentions, he'd let her down.

"Are you free?" He shoved his hands in his pockets, not breaking her stare.

"Free as a bird." There was no sense in pointing out the obvious. They were completely alone. For the first time ever, she was happy for the lack of business.

"Violet misses you," Ben said.

Disappointment landed square in her chest. "Well, I miss her, too," Mary said. "I'd be happy to still see her. She can stop by whenever she wants. But that's your decision."

Ben nodded. "She'd like that."

Mary chewed her lip, wondering if that was all he had to say, if he was just strolling by, and thought he'd ask. Her gaze drifted to the droplets of rain that had gathered on the shoulders of his wool coat. He didn't have an umbrella, and he was slightly out of breath. No one was out for a stroll today, and he hadn't bothered with a cab, it would seem. He'd run here. All this way. To see her.

She started to speak, to ask why he had come, if Violet was the only reason, but he started to speak at the same time, and they both stopped. Ben laughed nervously, and he held out his hand. "Ladies first."

This time she demurred. She needed to hear what he had to say. She had nothing left to say. Ben had made his decision. Or had he?

"Violet misses you," Ben repeated. His gaze tore through hers, as if he was contemplating his next sentence. "I miss you, too."

"Ben." Mary blinked, trying to process what he was saying, what it meant. If it changed anything.

He stepped forward, holding a hand up, and her heart began to hammer as he closed the distance between them, until she could smell the rain on his skin, feel the heat of his body, conjuring up all those memories of their night together that she'd tried so hard to push from her mind.

"Being with you . . . It scared me. I didn't know I could care about another woman again, I didn't realize I could imagine a future." He shook his head. "I pushed you away. It seemed easier than taking the chance on the unknown."

"But nothing's changed," Mary said. "The future is still unknown. Nothing is certain."

"Some things are. My love for my daughter . . . that's one. I want her to be happy. But I want to be happy, too. And these past few weeks since we've gotten to know each other have been some of the happiest days I've had in a long time."

Mary gave a small smile. "Same here."

"So what do you say?" Ben asked, his gaze turning hopeful. "Are you willing to give it another chance?"

Mary looked away as her mind began to whirr. It would be so easy to give in, to say yes, to fall back into that glorious place she'd found with him, but something had shifted, something had changed. That hope she'd felt, that joy, had been replaced with reality, and all its brutal possibilities.

She stole a glance at him, her heart softening a bit. Life was full of sweet possibilities, too.

She swallowed hard, trying to think with her head, not

her heart, to remember how it felt to love someone and to be left. To have that happiness ripped out from under you.

"I don't know, Ben." She shook her head, hating her words as much as she knew they were true. "I don't know if we can get back to that place. I dared to believe, you see, that this might be something special—"

"It was special," he said firmly. "It is special."

She sighed as she looked up at him. "I guess I don't know how I can stop myself from wondering if you'll do it again. Wake up one morning and have a change of heart."

He reached out and took her hand before she had a chance to snatch it back. He held it tightly, and oh, it felt so good. So right.

"I didn't have a change of heart," he said, his eyes pleading with hers. "I worried . . . that you might. Someday."

Mary shook her head, giving a bitter smile. "And here I thought this place was an issue. That you saw me as someone who could never give you the time you and Violet needed. Someone that had to work weekends and evenings."

He looked at her quizzically. "It's because of this place that my daughter smiled again. Don't ever think I wouldn't support your dreams."

Ben reached forward and wiped her lip with the pad of his thumb. He turned it over, smiling at the smear of chocolate.

Mary's lip still tingled from the sensation. She drew a sharp breath, sobering herself. She needed to be certain this time. She needed to be sure. If there was such a thing.

"This thing we have. You. Me. Anyone, really. It's a risk."

"I'm willing to take that risk if you are," he said, dropping her hand to slide his arms around her waist.

She smiled up into his eyes, listing to the rain pelt the windows. From somewhere in the distance the old jukebox was playing her favorite tune, again, as if her grandfather had arranged it that way, somehow.

Sunshine Creamery was empty, but standing here, in Ben's strong arms, her life had never felt fuller.

Some risks were worth taking.

# Epilogue

Mary and Violet were sitting on an old patchwork quilt in one of Mary's favorite shady corners in Lincoln Park, enjoying a "spot of tea" with mismatched plastic cups and saucers when Ben strolled up the path toward them, a long, cardboard tube tucked under his arm and a secretive smile teasing the corners of his mouth.

"Are those the plans?" Mary asked excitedly as she shifted to her knees.

Ben just gave a shrug as he dropped onto the grass beside them, nearly spilling the pitcher of fruit punch that Violet had helped make earlier. Mary tried to reach for the tube, but Ben masterfully maneuvered it out of reach.

Mary elbowed him. "Come on, let me see."

He leaned in, stealing a kiss instead, and despite her anticipation, Mary relaxed into the moment, savoring the sweet taste of his mouth.

"Ew!" Violet squealed, and then interrupted into a fit of giggles. "Kissing! Kissing!" She bent forward at the waist, laughing as if this were the funniest thing she'd ever seen. This was always her reaction when she caught them in the act, despite it being a more frequent occurrence, as Mary was pleased to note.

Pulling back, Mary and Ben watched her for a moment and then glanced at each other, falling into laughter themselves. "Come on, let me see," Mary said, nudging him again.

"Not until I hear your news," Ben said firmly. To drive home his point, his made a grand show of tucking the plans behind his back, far out of Mary's reach.

Mary sighed. She'd been holding in the announcement all day and now she felt as if she could burst. "Sam and Lila loved the idea. They said they couldn't have come up with something better themselves, actually. They think it's not just great for business, but also for marketing. A win-win, so to speak."

"Does that mean you're going to be driving an ice cream truck?" Violet asked excitedly.

"Only in the winter," Mary clarified. "But during the rest of the year I'll hire someone to do it for me."

Hire someone. She could barely even wrap her head around it. A mere month ago she was concerned she wouldn't make it another year, and now she was actually feeling secure enough to bring on a college kid to help drive her food truck. Sam had helped her crunch the numbers, and with the extra sales she should pull in from the food truck, not to mention the uptick in sales it should bring to Sunshine Creamery's main store, growth was now a realistic possibility.

"It's a brilliant idea," Ben said.

Mary took his hand across the picnic blanket. "And it was all yours."

"No, it was both of us," he said firmly. "But good things happen when you let people in."

Mary felt her eyes prickle with happy tears. She looked up at the sky, where not a cloud was in sight. It was a beautiful day, full of sunshine, laughter, warmth from the inside out. It was not a day for tears. Even the happy ones.

"Now it's your turn," she said.

Ben's eyes danced as he rubbed his hands together, dragging out the moment, and finally reached for the paper tube. He took his time rolling off the rubber bands and unveiling the detailed rendering of the three-story house with tall arched windows and a walk-out deck.

"Which one is my room?" Violet asked eagerly, crawling around on the blanket until she was wedged between them.

Ben pointed to a room at the back of the house, with a big bay window. "That one. You'll have a view of the yard, though I have to set your expectations a bit lower and say it's more like a patch of grass, being a city lot and all."

"And which one is yours?" Violet asked.

Ben exchanged a knowing smile with Mary and tapped his finger on the biggest room in the house, with large windows on two walls. "Mary thought this one was best for me. So I'd always have sunshine."

"What about Mary?" Violet asked, looking up at her. "Are you going to live in our house, too?"

Mary blushed and looked away, stumbling over her words as she tried to think of a tactful excuse. "Oh, honey, this is your house—"

Ben's hand was on hers, warm and firm, sure and steady. She felt her breath catch and she looked up into his deep, cloudy blue eyes and felt her heart warm on his smile.

"What do you think about that?" he asked, as casually as if he were suggesting a pizza for dinner, which he would, she was sure, before the day was through.

Mary blinked as she processed what he was asking, knowing that it would lead to something she'd thought she once lost and now had somehow found again. A family. With Ben and his sweet little girl.

"I think these past few months have shown me that anything is possible." She smiled up into his face as she flung her arms around his neck and gathered Violet in for a squeeze too. "Yes," she cried. "A thousand times, yes."

*Coming Soon*

## NO SWEETER LOVE

*Can friendship lead to forever?*

Claire Wells just helped the only man she's ever loved choose an engagement ring…for another woman. With her heart in pieces and her professional life in shambles, she turns to the one man she can always count on: her best friend. Ethan is more than just a shoulder to cry on—he's sweet, and funny, and okay, easy on the eye. In many ways, he's the perfect guy…aside from the fact that she's looking for forever and he's just looking for fun.

Ethan Parker is all too aware of his reputation as a ladies man. Inviting Claire to pose as his date for his cousin's wedding seems like the perfect solution for them both—she needs a break from the city and he needs to show his family that he's fully capable of committing to one woman. The trouble is, the more he pretends that Claire is his girlfriend, the more impossible it becomes to view her as just a friend…

Olivia Miles is a bestselling author of contemporary romance. A city girl with a fondness for small town charm, Olivia enjoys highlighting both ways of life in her stories. She currently resides just outside Chicago with her husband, daughter, and two ridiculously pampered pups.

Olivia loves connecting with readers. Please visit her website at www.OliviaMilesBooks.com to learn more.

56000578R00122

Made in the USA
Lexington, KY
09 October 2016